WEX

FOLK
TALES

WEXFORD
FOLK
TALES

BRENDAN NOLAN

The
History
Press
Ireland

For Nana, who lived her own story

First published 2013

The History Press Ireland
50 City Quay
Dublin 2
Ireland
www.thehistorypress.ie

ISBN 978 1 84588 766 7

Typesetting and origination by The History Press

CONTENTS

INTRODUCTION

Folklore is not history. It is history of a sort, but it is more the history of how people saw matters as it suited them at any time. Historians must be accurate in their records, that is important, but the folklorist gathers stories that in the telling show as much about the teller as they do the story told. People's perspectives change in the telling of a story. The further away from danger we travel the braver we become in the telling. The smallest achievement becomes a heroic deed. The omission fades in the telling until it was never there at all. The timid become tigers with the safety of time. The silly antagonist becomes sillier as fear of retribution and rebuke fade away.

It has often been observed that historians spend a great deal of their time contradicting one another and it is little wonder that they do so, for if you put two people on a stand to tell what they witnessed you will get three versions of the story: one from each and a third version that both agree is incorrect. This from people who were for the most part not there when the incident they are arguing about took place in the first place; but who are happy to argue about it as if they own what happened themselves as part of their personal treasure.

Storytellers just get on with the telling of the true story no matter the shade of circumstance. If someone in a story is terrified it matters not to them what day of the calendar it might be in a more leisurely circumstance.

There is a story told of a Wexford man who owned a bicycle, a black Raleigh Rudge with a Brooks saddle, as many people do and did, for getting to and from the nearest town. He loved his bike and declared he would use his present machine for as long as it would last, and that would be that.

The tyres wore out over the bumpy miles and he replaced them; the spokes bent and the wheels became bockety in potholes and he replaced the wheels, or had them repaired well enough for his purpose, which was the same thing. People noted all this and wondered at the life that was in that bike and its owner. When the chain grew so old and rusted that it parted from itself one time too many and even a new split-link would not remedy the situation, they were sure he would have to admit defeat and buy a new bicycle.

However, the solution was a simple one, as it is in most stories. The man lived at the foot of the hill into town, as his people had lived for centuries before him. And over time his body had grown slower and older so that by this stage he was no longer able to pedal the bike up the hill anyway; so he took to walking himself and his bike up the hill to conduct his business in the town. Once there, he took to throwing the bike in a ditch while he was away. It was an easy matter for him to retrieve the chainless bike on the way back, for nobody would steal a bike they could not pedal. Transport retrieved once more, the aged cyclist threw his good leg over the bike, pushed off with his spare foot and freewheeled down the hill, with his messages hanging from the handlebar – having no need whatsoever for a chain or pedals to get him there safely and in due course.

This collection of stories is like that man, if it resembles anything. The stories are here to enjoy but a printed story is no more than a butterfly caught in time. They must be released in the telling. Many of the stories in this book owe their origin to stories held in the Irish Folklore Commission Collection. Many were collected by schoolchildren in 1930s Ireland in a scheme devised by the Honorary Director of the Irish Folklore Commission, James Hamilton DeLargy.

The stories as collected and archived are necessarily brief, and are here extended using the skill of the present storyteller to fit the space allocated in this volume. Where a story from that collection is used, acknowledgement is made of the fine collectors and recorders. Some, unsurprisingly, seem to be tall enough tales told by a grandparent's generation to young eager ears, others are chilling and are as accurate, it seems, as if the older person was seeing it all happening before them, once more.

Where a number of stories were on the same subject and the integrity of the telling lent itself to some assistance, several stories are told together in the shape of a frame story on the subject, which is a technical matter or a trick of the storyteller's art, if you like. If it has been done properly a happy reader should see the whole as story woven from many threads.

Lots of the stories come from other sources and are included here for their integrity and fun at the foibles of man and his circumstance.

There are as many stories in this collection as there are days in the longest of months. They are here for you when you are in need of a story to laugh at, think on or disbelieve. Pick a story for yourself at random, sit up on your bike and freewheel all the way to the end of the book.

Safe travelling and mind the dark bend at the foot of the hill where the woman in the flowing dress and the cloak await you, for she too has a story to tell, if you dare listen.

Brendan Nolan, 2013
www.irishfolktales.com

One

THREE GEESE

Wexford folklorist Patrick Kennedy told the following tale of wandering geese and a wife who was nearly buried alive:

A tailor and his wife lived alone in a small cottage. They had no children but had lived a quiet and contented life for many years – until one day they had a difference of opinion over the number of geese marauding around their small garden.

The wife declared that there were at least a hundred geese trampling down their crop of oats and demanded that her lazy husband do something about it. He husband, who was busily pursuing his tailoring trade, pointed out (not altogether unreasonably) his good wife had less to do than he; but, rather than engage in an argument he knew he could not win, he rose with a sigh and headed out to deal with the reported invasion.

He stepped into the bright sunlight and was brought up short – all he could see was a pair of geese. One, two. This he reported to his wife (though perhaps he would have been better off not saying anything). Challenged, his wife amended her hand to fifty geese; but the tailor said he wished he was as sure of receiving 50 guineas as he was sure there were only two geese in it. She then declared that there were forty geese there, destroying the oats, as sure as there was one.

Giving up the argument on whether there was two, forty, fifty or a hundred, the tailor drove away the geese and went back to his tailoring, thinking all was well. But, when dinner came, after his wife had tumbled out the potatoes for him, placed a noggin of milk and a plate of butter before him, she went and sat in the corner by herself. With a dramatic gesture, she threw her apron over her head and began sobbing loudly.

The surprised tailor implored her to come over and take her dinner. But she was adamant there had been at least a score of geese in the garden when he had insisted there were only two, and that she would not sup with him until he owned to the truth. He stubbornly maintained that he owned to the truth, that there were two geese there and that was that.

The die was cast and the wife, instead of taking to the bed, made a shake-down for herself to lie on and would not gratify the tailor by sleeping in their high-standing bed beside him.

If the tailor thought a night's sleep would change her demeanour, he was mistaken. The following morning she would not rise, even after he had spoken kindly to her and brought some breakfast to where she lay. Instead, she asked him to go for her mother and relations; she wanted to take leave of them before she died. There was no use her living any more, not now all the love was gone from her marriage.

The tailor asked what he had done to bring their lives to this pass. His wife replied that he insisted there were only two geese in the garden when at the very least there could not be less than

a dozen. She demanded he acknowledge the truth and not to
be an obstinate pig of a man, and to let them be peaceful again.

Instead of giving her any answer, the tailor walked over to
her mother's house, and brought her back, with two or three of
her family, to take up the struggle on his behalf. But whatever
way words were exchanged, she near enough persuaded them
that her husband was to blame.

The tailor was called and was addressed by his declining
wife before the assembled mediators. She said that if he didn't
intend to send her to her grave, he should speak the truth and
agree that there were three geese there; though she persisted in
her assertion that there were six, at the very least, present. The
annoyed tailor refused to yield – there were but two. At that,
his wife told them all to go home, and on the way bid Tommy
Mulligan prepare her coffin. He was to bring it to the house at
sundown.

It's not everyday that someone orders their own coffin to
be brought to their wake; but thinking that doing so might
give her a fright, her kinspeople went to Tommy Mulligan and
brought back a coffin he had readymade for someone else that
was not quite dead yet. It was so new there were fresh shavings
in the bottom of the box. Once it was in the house, the tailor
took a wood auger to it and drilled some air holes in the coffin
lid, just in case.

Meanwhile, the gathered women ordered the men out so
they could wash the 'corpse', as was traditional. The tailor's
wife waited until the men were gone before she gave tongue to
the women – how dare they think she wanted or needed wash-
ing? If she chose to die, she said, it was no concern of theirs; if
anyone attempted to lay a drop of water on her, she would lay
the marks of ten nails on their face.

Just the same, washed or unwashed, she was persuaded to
get into the coffin, as a corpse might do. A clean cap and frill

was put around her face and her skin was attended to with sprinkled flour to give it a deathly pallor.

But while she was alive and not yet dead, the tailor's wife would have the last word on her appearance and when she saw her face in the mirror she took a towel and scrubbed the flour from it, restoring her rosy cheeks. She bid her husband be called in, and gave her sister and mother a charge, in his hearing, to be kind to the poor man after she was gone. However, she once again turned to the subject of the three geese and, without a word, the tailor put on his hat and walked out.

That was that. Evening came, and candles were lit, tobacco and pipes were laid out for mourners, and the night-long conversations commenced. They followed the usual themes and the poor undead woman had to listen to a good deal of conversation not to her liking. They discussed the cause of her death and the evidence that could be seen of it on her blotched skin (even though the corpse looked very well). They discussed her auld bitter tongue and the opinion was expressed that the tailor would bear her loss with patience. That he was a young man for his years – he didn't look forty – and he could have his pick of the village women. They tried to recall who it was that the tailor used to walk out with on an odd Sunday evening, before his marriage, and if that friendship could be resurrected within a few weeks of the funeral?

All this time the tailor's wife's blood was rushing around her veins like a herring caught in a net; but she was determined to die, out of spite, and she neither opened her eyes nor her mouth.

A broken-hearted tailor, in his misery, came up after some time and, leaning over her, whispered to be done with the foolery. If she would but say the word he, as her husband, would send all the people away about their business. But until he would admit that there were more geese in the garden than he claimed, his wife would not move and, giving up, the tailor went and sat in a dark corner of the room until dawn broke.

He made another offer next morning, just as the lid was being put on the coffin and the men were about to hoist it on their shoulders; but not a foot she would move unless he would give in to the three geese, which he would not.

They came to the churchyard, and the coffin was let down into the prepared grave. The tailor slid down to the coffin on his backside and, stooping to speak through the auger holes in the lid, he begged her, even after the holy show she had made of herself and himself, to give up the point and come home. All he got from her was the same question.

Every man has his breaking point and the tailor seemed to have reached his. He clambered up out of the grave, and began to shovel soil like mad down onto the coffin that he had lately stood upon.

The first loud rattle that the soil made on the bare lid nearly frightened the life out of the not dead woman. She shouted out to let her up, let her up, that she was not dead at all. She would even agree to there being only two geese if they would just let her up.

But the enraged tailor said it was too late; people had come from far and near to the funeral and they shouldn't be losing their day for nothing. So, for the credit of the family, he told his wife not to stir, and down went the soil in showers, for the tailor had lost his senses and who could blame him?

The bystanders, tiring of the sport, would not let the poor woman be buried against her will; so they seized the tailor and his shovel and restrained him. When his madness was checked, and he looked around at the concerned faces of the assembled crowd, he gave a low moan and collapsed on the ground in a dead faint.

When his wife stepped from the coffin, the first sight she saw was the tailor lying there, without a stir in him. A mischie-

vous neighbour proposed to her that she should let the tailor be put down in her place, and not give so many people a disappointment after coming so far to witness a burial. But the dead woman, now full of love for her marriage and understanding husband, was having none of it. She roared and bawled for the poor tailor to come to life, promising that if he did she'd never say a contrary word to him again while she lived. The tailor was brought around; but it took a good while for him to come around to looking his wife in the face after that.

Ever after, whenever a sharp answer came to tongue, the memory of rattling clods on a coffin and of the three geese that were only two after all came to mind, and her words were checked.

For such is the way that a tailor minds his own oats.

Two

THE STRANGENESS OF TEA

It is hard to think of a storytelling session that does not include the imbibing of tea, for it is never far from the lips of listeners and storytellers. It was not always so, for tea was a rarity in the Ireland of long ago. It was first consumed as a luxury item on special occasions, such as religious festivals, wakes, and family celebrations.

Folklorist Patrick Kennedy tells the tale of a Wexford farmer, 'Jemmy', who called at his landlord's house one day on business. He had drunk more than one jug o' punch in his time, but had not known the taste of tea between his teeth. He was kindly enough received by one of the young ladies of the house, who thought she could not offer him a more acceptable treat than a cup of tea.

She filled a large china cup, laid the sugar bowl beside it, and said, 'There, Jemmy, sweeten it to your liking,' as if he was well used to such things; he was not and he misunderstood her kind suggestion, and so left the sugar bowl untouched. The lady was called out of the room and the farmer, left alone, tentatively brought the cup of unsweetened tea to his lips and took a sip. This was his first taste of tea – and it was not to his liking. Horrible contortions passed over the man's features at the bitterness of the brew, but, out of politeness, he forced himself to empty the cup.

At home that evening he told his family and friends what had befallen him in the big house. All wondered how the upper classes could come to relish such disagreeable stuff.

Calling to the house again half a year later, he met a similar reception from the same young lady who once more thought he might like some tea. His hostess stayed in the room this time, so throwing the contents behind the fire or out of the

window was not an option. Jemmy fearfully eyed the cup and when it was filled put the vessel to his mouth as a child would a cup of medicine; but this time the young lady, identified only as Miss C., had added the sugar herself and stirred it for him with a delicate hand.

Like a great many before him and since, Jemmy was agreeably surprised by the pleasant taste of the beverage. After draining every drop with the highest relish, he laid the cup down, and addressed his kind host. 'Many thanks, Ma'am, for that nice drink. What do you call it?'

'That is green tea, Jemmy.'

'Ah then, Ma'am, the love of my heart was the green tay, but to Halifax with that stuff that you sweeten to your liking.'

At least Jemmy was lucky enough to drink tea from a person who knew how to make it. When tea first came to Wexford and the rest of the country many people did not know what to do with it. Some used to put the tealeaves into the teapot, poured boiling water over them, left them to brew and then, throwing out the water, tried to eat the leaves with sugar sprinkled over them. On the Blasket Islands off Kerry the first shipwrecked tea to wash ashore was used to die homemade clothes.

On another occasion, a country clergyman hired a new housekeeper and handed her a paper of tea the first evening of her service, with directions to prepare it as soon as was convenient. She was rather long about the business, but at last made her appearance with two plates, one bearing a darkish mass of damp leaves, the other a pat of butter.

'Musha, your reverence, but this new kind of cabbage is mighty hard to boil tender. Put butter to your own taste in it; I didn't know how you'd like it.' To the reader of this story this might seem to be a fair compromise. But the clergyman saw it otherwise.

'Well, indeed, I am afraid I won't like it with or without butter,' he said. 'But if you relish it yourself, you're welcome to it.' For the clergyman loved his tea in the usual way, boiled in a pot and served in a cup. No doubt he took a hand in his cook's culinary education in the days that followed.

Tea was to feature in another story of a woman who set her cap at someone who was somewhat above her own station in life.

Nora was a healthy, bouncing, young country maiden, but was in no way gifted with outstanding beauty. One day she vowed that she would be the wife of young Mr Bligh, a 'half sir' (whatever that was) who lived nearby. The young man always spoke civilly and good-naturedly to her, but after a year or two's application to her task Nora saw no immediate sign of holding to her.

So she held consultations with those who were expert in enchantment lore and was interested to discover that the liver of a thoroughly black cat was sovereign in the process of pro-curing a return of love. It was not something that would have occurred naturally to her, or to few others for that matter.

Aided by her sister and by another woman, a suitable, if unwilling, cat was slain with the prescribed accompaniments. The liver was carefully taken out, broiled, and reduced to an impalpable powder, according to Patrick Kennedy who had made a study of the story, if not the cat itself. In a day or two the brave half sir was passing by Nora's cottage and, seeing her at the gate, he stopped to chat with her.

Delighted with this turn of events, Nora kept up the con-versation and, after some further talk, asked might she take the liberty of requesting him to come in and take a cup of tea? He did not want to do so, for he had some indication by now that Nora was more enamoured of him than he of her. But he felt he could not refuse the invitation without incivility, so he allowed himself to be seated comfortably at the table, making as much small talk as he thought appropriate. Nora soon filled his cup from a blackened teapot, which, in addition to some indifferent tea, contained a pinch of the philtre all three women had made up from the cat's innards.

The guest sat down with notions not very complimentary to his entertainer; but when he took up his hat to walk home, he was lost in love. Moreover, he was determined on setting her up as the mistress of his heart and house, such was the potency of the drink he had imbibed. Powerful stuff indeed.

However, nothing lasts forever and it is in the nature of this magic potion that if the dose is not repeated at intervals the effect becomes weaker and, at length, will cease altogether. Nora, aware of this, renewed the administration at every visit until his infatuation became such that he announced to his family and relations his immediate intention to marry the cottage girl.

This was a surprise to many. Fruitless were the coaxings, threats and reasonings that were put to him, until at last the eve of the wedding day arrived. Paying a visit to his soon-to-be wife on that happy evening, they soon fell to talking and laughing like lovers did, oblivious to what was about to happen. They were enjoying the most interesting and delight-ful conversation that was ever exchanged between a man and a woman when the latch was raised on the door of the cottage, and a party of seven or eight young men armed with good strong hazel rods entered and began to lay blows on the back and shoulders of the groom-to-be.

Nora flung herself between the attackers and her nearly-husband, and received a few slight blows in passing for her earnestness. Before they ceased beating the amorous youth, every bone in his body was sore. He was unable to use either his arms or his legs and they carried him away from the cottage of enchanted love. They bundled him into a car and took him home, where he was tended and watched over for a full month of the calendar. Nora and her cat's tea were kept away from him and she was denied access to the love of her life.

As time passed the effect of the drug began to wear off, so much so that when the young man was at last able to quit his bed he was amazed that he should ever have been guilty of such an absurdity as to consider marrying a woman over a cup of tea.

As for Nora, we don't know what happened to her when the story ended but it is unlikely that, once she had mastered the preparation of cat's tea, she would have wasted it on anything but a fine catch for herself.

It might be as well if you are out walking and are offered a cup of tea by a woman named Nora in Wexford that you might first enquire, for your own sake, if she keeps cats.

Three

CAT
KILLER

The following tale was gathered from Mrs Furlong of Wexford in 1938 by William Saddler, a pupil at Wexford Christian Brothers' School, whose memory of the original story is stored in the Irish Folklore Commission Collection.

A man by the name of Sir Walter Whitty was to be married to one Lady Devereux of Ballymaghery. It seems that neither was a person of great means, for the bride thought it would be a fine idea for her groom to go and kill a few rabbits for the wedding feast.

It would have been the easiest thing in the world for him to pay a local man to catch a few rabbits; many parts of Wexford were well-populated with rabbits and they were easily got. Rabbit meat was a commodity that could be traded for other goods and rabbit skins fetched good prices in their own right. Trapping was best done at night, when rabbits were unsuspecting of approaching death. A noose was made out of strong, slim wire and was attached to a wooden peg driven into the ground. This was placed across a rabbit run so when an unsuspecting rabbit next made its way along the track its head would slip inside the noose, which would tighten on its neck. In the very early morning, trappers could often be seen coming into town with their prizes from the night before hanging from poles carried on their shoulders.

Catching rabbits was a skill passed down in communities and through families in the Wexford countryside, but it was not a personal skill possessed by Sir Walter. Nonetheless, he did his best to meet the wishes of his bride-to-be, for he would not let anyone except himself hunt rabbits for his marriage feast. Sir Walter took himself off to the burrows to see how he might get on. He hunted all day, but never a rabbit could he catch for he had neglected to bring any snares with him. His plan was to stun any rabbit he saw with a well-flung stone from his strong right hand.

Whether his plan would have worked in practise was never put for the test, for although he waited all day he never saw a rabbit to take aim at. Several times he was about to strike when he realised the four-legged animal slinking through the grass was not a rabbit but one of the many cats that were to be found in the area. Several paused and watched the man before them, as quietly and intently as they might watch a mouse who had no means of escape from a waiting feline.

Sir Walter stayed there for hours and exchanged greetings as nonchalantly as he could with any passers-by, a few of whom stopped to wish him well on the morrow on the occasion of his marriage to Lady Devereux. Any of the men would have been happy to advise him on rabbit catching, for a sir would be a useful person to have indebted to you. Most of the men could do anything, from poaching a salmon to thatching a roof to

catching rabbits to sell or eat, so they would have made ready instructors. But pride comes before a fall and a proud man can starve to death in the midst of plenty when he will not ask for assistance from another human being.

Finally, as night fell, Sir Walter admitted defeat and set off on his journey home empty handed. After a while on the road, he left people and houses behind him. It became so quiet as he walked that there was hardly a noise to be heard, only the sound of his own heart beating and his breath rising and falling, and by now it was nearly pitch dark. Cresting the top of a hill near his home, a sudden shiver ran through his body, as if a pickpocket had taken all belonging to him in one go.

He glanced over his shoulder as quickly as he could, though there was no sound coming from that quarter. He saw the impression of the empty road he had just travelled along, he saw the bank on either side and he saw the trees a little way behind him that, when he had started, were before him. Just as he was about to turn back and continue his journey home, he spotted, out of the corner of his left eye, a faint white impression. Was it a ghost? A thief come to rob him? He focussed directly at the spot and his fright and confusion became realisation and annoyance when he saw it was only a large white cat perched on a bank of sand at the side of the dark road. It was alone, it was a huge animal and it was motionless. It recorded with its unblinking eye his every shift, and every nuance of his frame. His next breath reached the bottom of his lungs for there is nothing more energised than a man whose terror has been assuaged. Sir Walter's knightly head and neck stretched out of his coat like an angry goose disturbed by approaching footfall.

He remembered the cats of earlier in the day; the cats he thought must have chased away the rabbits and prevented him from obtaining his prize; the cats who had sat staring at him, mocking him, as he had waited in vain for his opportunity to strike. He shouted to the night air that he wished bad luck to the cat and to all its breed, seed and generation. Not content with that, he kicked the ground and disturbed a stone, which tinkled away from his foot in the darkness. Though it was as dark as the hobs of Hell on that road he was still able to pick up the stone in his right hand. The cat, though unmoved by the curses rained down on it by the man, flicked its tail when he saw the arm raised above his head, but by then it was too late. The fair-sized stone left the man's fist, flew through the night air and struck the white cat squarely on the forehead, killing it instantly. It fell without sound or protest.

Sir Walter left the body where it had fallen and travelled on. He had crested the highest point of the journey before he met the watching cat and the road now fell away beneath his feet. The hurrying knight was not long about reaching his dwelling place. He entered, slammed the door behind him and went to where a large log fire lay smouldering in the grate. He shook off his damp outdoor clothes and sat down to remove his top-boots and the cloth overalls wrapped round his legs. He was cold and he was hungry and on the morrow there was going to be less food for his guests at the promised wedding breakfast. He would also have to answer to his new wife on his inability to provide. It did not seem to him to be a propitious start to any venture, much less a marriage to a lady. He heaved the sigh of a frustrated man.

He glanced up and saw the cat of the household sitting in front of him, disturbed from its recent reverie beside the fire. Another cat! He could not get away from them. He stared at the cat for a time before he spoke. The cat stared back. Sir Walter spoke to the cat in Barony of Forth language so that the old cat might better understand. He said the words: 'Maude killed Jude,' which apparently meant 'Cat, I killed your kitten.'

Sir Walter barely had the words out of his mouth when the old cat arched her back, stood upright, bared her teeth and sprang straight at the knight. He was alone in the room, and before anyone could hear what was happening, the old cat had cut the man's throat open to allow his life blood to flow away.

If the white cat died instantly out in the darkness of the road, so too did the errant knight before the dying log fire. When the servants hurried into the room in response to his terrified death shriek, they were already too late. They could not see the cat anywhere and wrongly assumed that it was a devil that had attacked their late employer.

There was no wedding of course, not only were there no rabbits to eat but there was now no groom to guide matters along. His bride-to-be, Lady Devereux, hearing of her lover's death, drowned herself in the well of the garden of her home. Her ghost was to be seen for years afterwards walking about the grounds of her family home dressed in white, waiting for a wedding that never came.

And, from that night to this, the spectre of Sir Walter Whitty may be seen sitting in the hall of his family home with a ghost cat stuck at his throat, its teeth bared and its claws open.

Four

A Soft
Step

Patrick Kennedy gathered the following story in his 1869 work *Evenings in the Duffrey*.

At the beginning of the nineteenth century, in the Castledockrell area, there stood a large old manor house that rose to three storeys in height, at a time when housing stock generally managed to rise no more than a single floor above the earth. A young man lived there who was neither noble in thought nor deed, nor concerned in the slightest with the lives of the people who lived around him, save for the occasional fresh young woman to play with.

Alaster Henry found every opportunity to plámas any likely lady his eye fell upon, and to tell them how beautiful and amusing and wise beyond their years they were. At the time of this story there were two servant girls working in his home: Oonagh Matthews and Peggy Devereux. Oonagh was smooth-faced and a handsome young girl, by all accounts, but light in the head and fond of flattery. Peggy was neither so handsome nor so light-headed.

There also lived on his land an old woman who went by the name of Shebale who, for whatever reason, agreed to be used more than once by the master for his purposes. She was a useless woman, good for nothing but causing trouble in other's lives. When the master had no use for her he treated her like he would one of the dogs that wandered about the yard, ushering her out of his way or ignoring her altogether, which made her all the more determined to be of service to him.

She knew the master had set his eye on Oonagh and took it upon herself to lay siege to the unsuspecting girl on his behalf. She hinted that Oonagh might have the chance of being the mistress of the Big House some day, though she never said how this was to come about. And, Shebale promised, if the match was indeed made her father would not outlaw her for marrying the master.

A tenant's son, Charley Kenny, who worked at the harder tasks for the house, was meanwhile in love with Oonagh. She was aware of his feelings and sometimes encouraged him and other times gave him the cold shoulder, according to whether she had lesser or greater hopes of becoming Master Henry's wife one day.

On the other hand, Peggy felt a great and continuing liking for Charley; but, he only respected her for her good sense and conduct. Peggy knew she had no hope there while Oonagh was first in his eye.

The machinations of Alaster Henry went on for some time, now paying the girl attentive court and then wandering away from her after some alternative interest until she did not know when, if ever, she would become his wife and mistress of the house. She said so to Shebale the schemer, whenever they were alone, but the cunning old woman always turned the conversation back to whether Oonagh would be happy to be mistress of the Big House with all the responsibilities that would entail.

Oonagh confided in Peggy that she had high hopes for the future, without saying what these hopes were based upon or what they might be. Peggy advised her to keep her mind on her own company and to notice that Charley Kenny had an eye for her. He would inherit the tenant's job and cottage when his parents died. He would make a good husband and provider for a family, said Peggy to her uncaring work mate.

Spring rolled into summer and summer's luscious ways gave way to autumn when the roads were strewn with leaves, and winter dawned when ardour should have been tempered by the quietness of the land and the cold winds flowing around the eaves of the big house. Oonagh's impatience at the progress of her wooing by the master grew and grew, but the more it grew the less heed he paid to her.

All Hallows' Eve arrived. Unbeknownst to Oonagh, Alaster Henry and Shebale had held two or three conversations before this night came along and had hatched a plan.

There was a plentiful table spread that evening for the servants and labourers in the big kitchen. There was a fire in the hearth large enough to roast an ox and the plates and dishes on the big dresser were shining in the blaze from the fire. The mother of Alaster came and sat by the kitchen fire and talked with the servants about their families, and everything that was happening in the townlands about them. Everyone was cheerful enough to be in out of the cold, enjoying the warmth and the plenty before them.

Once the food had been eaten the traditional games of the night began. These included trying to match men with women in marriage and boys and girls in romance. They laughed when one wag tried to match Shebale with a seventy-year-old man who they said had a further thirty years of life in him yet. She reacted to the taunting by offering to take her tormentor's nose off with the red-hot fire tongs.

Thwarted with Shebale, Thumkin (the master of ceremonies) turned on Charley Kenny and Peggy Devereux for a match, to not much success either. Peggy blushed, and laughed, and asked him to stop, but he kept on with the attempt. Charley, not realising that Peggy was blushing for him, bounced away in half a minute, all interest gone. Shebale took the opportunity to whisper to Oonagh, whom she was sitting beside, that she would put in a match for her and the master to see how it came out. She had prepared the game beforehand to achieve the desired result and when it came out that way, Oonagh nearly fainted from the proof set before her on this night of tradition, folklore and belief.

Thumkin saw what had transpired and asked of Shebale who the happy couple were? She replied that she would not tell and she and Oonagh sat in quiet peace as the revelry and ri-rá continued about the high-ceilinged kitchen for the rest of the evening.

All fell silent in time and the party ended. Some slipped quietly out into the dark night like lost souls, some protested the passing of the company and went off hallooing into the night seeking their own reflection. Finally, there was no one left in the kitchen but Oonagh, Shebale, and Cáit, a young kitchen helper.

Peggy had decided not to share their settle-bed that night with Oonagh, for she realised that something was afoot that she did not want to be a part of. She said she would prefer to go home with her brother. Charley Kenny said he would keep them company in the walk home, which pleased her more than whatever Oonagh was cooking up with the old woman in the corner.

Oonagh asked eagerly what was in store for her following the night's revelations. Shebale told her to be off, herself and little Cáit, to the place of the meeting of the stream and the river, where three townlands met, and gave her instructions on what to do when she was there. The two left the house and were off across the fields before the door had settled in its frame behind them.

Peggy and her company took the long way home, for when they got to the top of the avenue, instead of turning up the lane to the left, which would have brought them home to their own village, they took the right-hand turn to see a young girl, a friend of theirs, safe at home at her mother's cabin – for no one, boy or girl, would care to be out by themselves on All Hallows' Eve. Peggy was pleased at the detour for it prolonged her time with Charley. When they were halfway back again, Charley noticed a couple of girls flitting by inside the field. Curious, he said farewell to his companions and leapt over the ditch into the field himself. He followed them on across the field, through another field, and along a path that crossed a hill, till they came out where the stream fell into the river from a little height.

The pair were frightened enough, but determined in their work. Oonagh took out from under her cloak a whitish piece of cloth, which Charley guessed was one of her shifts, and, after looking about in a tremble, drew it three times up the stream, and three times down the stream, to attract her lover, and then she and Cáit left the bank to return whence they came.

Charley was sorry to see the girl he liked so well do a devilish thing, which he knew was a mortal sin. Still, he was prepared to give her the benefit of the doubt if it was out of love for himself that she had done it. He resolved to have her opinion on it on the morrow and give her up forever if she did not make him a pleasant answer.

Back in the kitchen once more, the shivering girls found the fire still kept alight by Shebale. A small table was covered with a clean cloth and a cake was laid out on it. Oonagh spread the wet shift on the back of a chair before the fire, and climbed into the settle-bed beside old Shebale who lay where Peggy should have been. Cáit went off to find a warm corner for herself and the room quietened.

Still trembling from her evening's adventures, Oonagh covered up her head and never stirred till she heard the latch of the door lifted. Peeping out, she saw the young master walk slowly and stately across the stone floor towards the fire in a white linen vestment with close-fitting sleeves, reaching nearly to the ground.

After standing quite still beside the chair, the figure took Oonagh's shift in his hands, turned it on the back of the chair, and after another little delay, sat down at the table. He broke a piece of cake slowly, and put it in his mouth, and then got up to turn his face towards an enchanted Oonagh as she lay beside the old woman, almost too fascinated to breath. With a faint smile on his lips he walked out in the same silent way he had come. He might have been a ghost for all the noise he made, as there was no sound from his step either in the coming or going of him. Oonagh followed as lightly in his tread.

On the morrow, Charley made time for a talk with his true-love but this time she met him with such coldness and dislike that he never gave her another opportunity of showing her importance as long as he lived.

Matters moved swiftly in the next twelvemonth. By the time the next Hallowe'en rolled around, Peggy Devereux was busy boiling the stirabout for Charley Kenny, her new husband, who had sense enough to make her his wife following their long chattering ramble in the dark with her brother.

Shebale passed away one day suddenly, without having had time to make her peace with God for all her machinations and the work of the Devil she had undertaken while alive.

As for Oonagh, instead of being Master Henry's wife and mistress of the mansion, she was nursing an infant on her own in the cabin of her heart-broken parents. She had time enough for reflection, for she no longer worked nor was welcome in the Big House.

Five

MARRIAGE OF A
MAN AND A WOMAN

There was a lot to be considered before rushing into marriage in the old days in Wexford. It was not for nothing that people said 'marry in haste, repent at leisure'. In an agrarian society great care was given to who was allowed to marry into the family, for the new member might one day become the owner of the family fortune (even if that fortune was only a few acres of land, a house and a few working animals). It was good if they came from a neighbouring holding as the union would see the extended family holding more land between them. Failing that, a bride's dowry would often clear a debt or ease the way to buying some land from a neighbour.

It was not for nothing that Liam Roche's mother, who had observed the comings and goings of nature (and magpies in particular), recalled that marriage is the third part of the old pishogue: it is one magpie for bad luck; two for good luck;

three for a wedding; four for a wake. Luck, marriage and death, in that order.

Liam's mother had been in the ground for a good few years and Liam was in his seventies with neither chick nor child to worry himself about, when he took a notion that he might like a young woman about the house, and a few children as well, to fetch things for him when he grew too old to move about with any speed.

He thought about the matter for a considerable time and asked a few other single men that he had been in with if there were any likely women in the locality that had a notion to marry? And, if so, who would he go to for to ask for her hand?

This news was met with consternation and incredulity by a good many of his bachelor confidants; for one of their rank to suddenly announce that he was considering crossing to the married man's side of the road was an unsettling experience. Few, if any of them, had foreseen or even contemplated that it might happen to one of them.

Nevertheless, they gave the matter some consideration. A dowry would be the deciding factor in this campaign, they all agreed with certainty. They went through the names of most of the women in the locality first, then in surrounding parishes, then throughout the county and, finally, the talk came to crossing the border into County Carlow. There was a notion among these men that the women of Carlow would be happier to marry a Wexford man than one of their one county men, a Wexford man being a prize catch for a Carlow woman seeking to better her station in life, or so they told one another with conviction, based on no evidence whatsoever. Consequently, a better settlement could be sought in the matter of a dowry by the Wexford man, and by Liam himself on this occasion – or at least by a man working on his behalf in the negotiations in the matter.

At that time there was a man named Sean who lived near Carna who was so inured of his wife's complaining over the years that he paid little heed to it, but one fine day, when he returned from the fields with his day's earnings in his pocket and she said for the umpteenth time that the husband next door was a better provider than the man standing before her, he decided that enough was enough. The next day, he travelled to Liam's home in Kilmore ,for he was a nephew by marriage of Liam. He explained his predicament and that no matter what he did he could not satisfy his wife or her brothers, his brothers-in-law. In the heel of the hunt, he borrowed the fare to New York from Liam and away he went, swearing Liam to secrecy. He had no need to do that for where money was concerned Liam was as inscrutable as the Sphinx beyond in Egypt. He would say nothing to anybody, lest they think he was not a poor farmer at all.

Sean the nephew took himself off and was never seen again by his carping wife or her brothers, though every month some dollars were sent anonymously to Liam from America to repay the loan.

The episode had coloured Liam's thoughts on what a good wife might make; still, he was not on his own in the adventure he had embarked upon. The Hopper Mahon, who had sat beside him in school, agreed to operate as his blackman, the name given to the negotiator in arranged marriages. It wasn't long before his old comrades had narrowed the field down to a few likely women, mostly from Carlow, and matchmaking began. The Hopper was engaged in the negotiations, which were surprisingly brisk, for although Liam thought he projected an image of a poor farmer the rest of the county knew him to be a snug man. And since he had the wheeze of a seventy-year-old man who is on the way down the far side of the hill, there was no shortage of unmarried women who would be happy enough to lie down in the bed with him, for a while anyway.

The only drawback that not even the Hopper Mahon could surmount was that to the woman, their childbearing days were behind them. So, Liam could have a wife but no children of his own with her. An alternative was that he could marry a widow who already had some children, but Liam said he could not countenance the thought of waking up and seeing another man's face peering at him through a child's features in the night. So that was out.

Now, not too far away lived a woman called Kate Murphy. Although getting on a bit in years, she was well liked and respectable. The reason she was unmarried was that she had cared for her ailing father beyond her marrying years. He died and the land went to her eldest brother who promised her a home for life; but then went and got married himself. The competition between women in this life is something that is rarely referred to in any overt way in polite company, at least outside of a court hearing on disputed land. But it is there and before long Kate was on the lookout for a berth of her own away from her gom of a brother and his new wife.

She soon enough heard about Liam's quest and made enquiries as to his standing. Satisfied, she made a point of crossing his track at the next market and asked his assistance to pass from one place to another over broken ground in safety.

The Hopper was soon in there and paid a visit to the Murphy household, where Kate's brother was only too happy to agree a settlement on her so that he could get some peace from his wife.

Liam was happy enough too, for Kate's eye had caught his when he had helped her when she almost tumbled over in front of him at the market. He remembered the feel of her firm body for a long time afterwards, and the shortness of breath he experienced when he let her go to stand on her own.

Matters proceeded well enough and they went to the church to arrange the formalities. The banns were to be called on three successive Sundays or holydays. The first Sunday the priest stood up and said: 'Let it be known to all here present that Liam Roche intends with God's grace to enter into the state of matrimony with Kate Murphy, if you know of any affinity, consanguinity or any spiritual relationship to prevent this marriage you are bound to make it known as soon as possible.'

Most proposed marriages face a challenge sooner or later and this one faced a challenge the following week from the unlikely quarter of Larry Brennan. One of Larry's sows had strayed during the week and, despite much searching, had still not been found by the following Sunday. Larry was sitting beside another man near the back of the church at 10 o'clock mass when the notices were being read out. He had driven the man next to him mad with his questions about the sow and in asking him to repeat everything the priest read out. Finally, when he asked one question too many the man, in exasperation, told him that a sow had been found and the priest was calling it out.

Larry Brennan immediately shouted out that the sow was his and repeated it twice, just in case there was any doubt in the congregation's mind as to what he had said. Tragically, the priest had just read out the bans between Liam and Kate for the final time when Larry began roaring.

All was confusion and everyone in the church was soon in uproar. For a while it looked as though Liam's hopes of marriage were over, and the Hopper had to move fast to prevent Liam from returning home for the pike in the thatch to run Larry Brennan through for his insult to Liam's wife-to-be. Eventually, things calmed down enough for the Hopper to explain to a bewildered Larry that the sow was still missing and that the priest did not have it. He persuaded Larry to go

his cousin's house in Lisdonvarna for a few weeks until the marriage was over, if he valued his life.

He then had the difficulty of re-negotiating the dowry with the Murphy lad who, egged on by his affronted wife, wanted to lessen the amount of dowry payable over the insult to his family's pride.

Finally all was settled and the marriage took place. The pike was surrendered to the Hopper by the newly-weds and peace of a sort descended on the love nest. But as to where the sow went (perhaps to Carlow or New York after the man from Carna) nobody was ever afterwards able to say, and the same sow was never heard of in that parish ever again.

Six

WIDOW
WOMAN

Death was usually how most couples were put asunder in an age when divorce was unheard of in Ireland. Sometimes women died in childbirth, leaving the widower with motherless children to care for until he tied the knot once more with a new wife. Other times, it was the man who passed away from some illness or other, or from a workplace accident in a time when most work was manual and safety non-existent. The state of widowhood was not a state most people aspired to, be they man or woman; but most men in need of marrying or re-marrying still shied away from a woman who had put not one, not two, but three husbands in the ground while she was still above it herself.

Biddy Horan had married three times, the first time to a man that she had something on, for she said he was the father of her unborn child. Whether he was or not, she declared shortly after the marriage was consummated in their little cottage that she was no longer with child, which confused her young husband, Maurice, no end. For he had thought he was starting a family with a new wife and instead found himself in a bed with a bony, snoring stranger lying beside him.

Maurice did not last long in marriage or in this life, and Biddy soon found herself with a neat little cottage on the edge of Maurice's people's land. It was here she stayed even when she married her second spouse, a stoker on a boat that sailed from Wexford to Wales. He was gone more often than he was home, and before long Biddy thought he might have another family in Wales at the other end of his sailing days. He was back and he was away, and then one day he was neither one nor the other – he was lost at sea. She was told one night he was on the boat and the next he was not, so it was assumed that a sea monster had come to take him away. His name was Noah; his family name is of no consequence for Biddy was born a Horan and a Horan she would remain, no matter how many men shared marriage vows with her.

Husband number three was a quiet man from Waterford by the name of Denis Murnaghan. He had a shock of red hair and a smile on him that put everyone in good humour when they met him. He saw the soft side of everything and the goodness in all. But Biddy got the best of him and she wore him down once they were married. He was led into marriage by his curiosity, but curiosity killed the cat and he was not long for this world.

He soon found that Biddy talked of nothing except outwitting people in making bargains, and how her father showed her how to pass off an old useless horse for a fresher one, or get a good price for a banjaxed pig. Biddy boasted of how she cheated customers when she worked in Kennedy's shop before she was married the first time: by passing off bad butter under the good, selling old eggs for fresh, and more besides which Mr Kennedy knew nothing about. This was all foreign to Denis and he longed for his carefree, unmarried days.

In the February following their marriage there was a heavy snow storm where they lived, and the snow was so deep on the ground that it came level with the tops of the fences. It was hard to know where anything was with only an undulating blanket of white blinding snow to be seen everywhere. People dug out paths along the roads to get to mass or to feed the sheep and cattle in the fields, and new-born lambs perished from the cold. The snow lay on the ground until April and Denis didn't get to see the thaw, as by this stage he had long been buried in the frozen ground. Some said it was from exhaustion trying to please Biddy all day long.

The night he died a high wind moaned and growled in the bare white trees. It was a night that might have frightened the bravest of men; but it took not a bother out of Biddy.

Before he was buried Denis was shaved, his open eyes were closed and his mouth was tied with a string to keep it shut until he was coffined. His clothes were removed and a habit was placed on his body. His arms were crossed and rosary beads were tied around his hands in case he might meet the Devil on his journey. Biddy gave his best Sunday clothes to a young man, as was the custom, and he dressed in the dead man's clothes and went out to walk in the snowy yard. He was not long gone before he returned and changed back out of them again, as tradition observed.

Biddy wore black once more, in memory of her recently deceased man, and inquired quietly after the sandy-haired lad that had worn Denis' clothes for her. He seemed nice and, as far as Biddy knew, was unattached. People stopped calling on her as the snow thawed. Work was there aplenty just waiting to be dug up. Some dug with enthusiasm, others with despair;

but the ground had to be uncovered. Meanwhile, the young man went off to stay with his aunt in California.

The snow departed but the earth was still cold and the nights were icy. A parsimonious Biddy mixed coal slack with cow dung into mortar balls to place at the back of the fire where they burned away slowly to give body to the few sods of turf she pegged in for good measure. The paraffin oil lamp that Noah the stoker had brought her from one of his voyages burned bright in the kitchen, but the well-married woman longed for company.

Then, just as darkness fell one evening, a man came into the farmhouse and asked to be put up for the night, if it was not too much of an imposition. Biddy said he could have the settle-bed beside the fire when she was retired herself. She told him she was recently widowed and he nodded gravely but said nothing, expressing neither sorrow nor sympathy for her loss.

Biddy looked at him closely, for he seemed familiar. He was clean-shaven and his face was thin. He had thin lips to match his face and his nose was also narrow and high. His black eyes were fixed on her from beneath heavy eyebrows as he took the strong, sweetened tea from her hands with fingers that were long and slender.

He told her his name was John Langan and that he hailed from Passage East on the Waterford side. She asked if he knew her late husband and fellow Waterford man Denis Murnaghan? He said he had heard the name and asked what sort of a man he was. She said he was the most innocent man that ever drew on a stocking; that he knew nothing and could be bested by anyone with a head on them.

Her visitor listened without taking his eyes from her lips even once and when she was done, John Langan was silent for a long time. Biddy then stayed quiet herself for a change, for she sensed the man was about to tell her something. When he spoke it was with a low and measured voice that gave resonance to each and every word he uttered.

He said he knew the man she meant. He put the fear of death into her by saying he had a message for her from him. He had stayed his hand until he was sure he was in the right house. Her late husband had not gone on yet and now had no means of earning his bread, for he was neither the one thing or the other; and his working clothes were nearly worn out, he said quietly, so quietly that Biddy leaned in closer to him to hear better. He was now begging at the doors of Christians for what he needed, she heard John Langan say.

The face on Biddy went whiter than the lime-washed walls outside ever could. She was afraid to speak. John Langan said her husband had bid him to tell her that if she'd send him a comfortable suit of clothes, not forgetting a pair of double-soled brogues he had left behind, she would make a man of him.

Biddy nodded in petrified agreement.

John Langan said Denis would also like an ass to carry him from one charitable house to another. If he had that he would be as happy as a king, for the animal would ease the burden to his poor legs.

Biddy was by now intoxicated with the wonder of it all. If John Langan had levitated before the fire she would have accepted it as no more than was natural. Her dead husband had sent for his clothes, and an ass. Imagine.

All that had been asked for would be ready bridled and saddled in the stable in the morning so the visitor could be away to him, she said. His full suit would be laid out by the kitchen table. She did not say it was the suit the America-bound man had worn the night Denis was waked in the parlour. She was not foolish. To test the water and see how far she needed to go she added that if John Langan thought it would be of any use, she could put some guinea notes in the pockets. But John Langan said no, that was not necessary and for that Biddy was relieved.

When Biddy rose the following morning it was to a deathly silence, inside and out. Her visitor was gone. Her only ass was gone and everything that Denis Murnaghan had brought with him to the marriage was gone from the house. It was as if he had never been. Of John Langan there was no trace, then or ever since.

Seven

140-YEAR-OLD MAN

Some men seem capable of living forever and would never have died were it not for some malice of nature or misunderstanding between men that end their lives prematurely, such was the case of a Wexford farmer who was the victim of a misunderstanding.

Máire Cait Ní Goc ,who in April 1935 was aged twenty-six years herself, told folklorist Jim Delaney of a man she had heard tell of who died prematurely at the early age of 140 years. Cait was a farmer's daughter residing in the parish of Bannow, or so the records in the Irish Folklore Commission collection above in Dublin testify.

A town was founded at Bannow during the early Norman period but has since disappeared for some reason. The old church of Bannow remained at the time of this story and was a fine ruin, lying near the island of Bannow, overlooking the sea. Most churches have a graveyard attached and this church was no exception. In its graveyard was purported to be the grave of the man who died at the age of 140 years. Sadly, we do not know his name nor whether he left any issue who might, even now, be striding through the county at a fine age. He is said to have married three times in his lifetime and was 100 years old the last time he swore to love his new wife until death did them part. It seems all three women pre-deceased him while he lived on into his second century of life and work on his Wexford farm.

He would have lived much longer than 140 years, save for what happened to him on a day he went to town to have something fixed for the farm.

We may suppose that his farmhouse was like most of the old stock that were built: constructed with mud-walls, firm and so high as to rise to a loft above the ground floor, which served as a warm bedroom with three walls, the missing wall being the one to the kitchen below it. In any case, it would have been neat and well-accommodated, with all necessary implements of the day for a comfortable life; for you do not live to that age by being sloppy or lazy in your life or surroundings, for laziness catches up on everyone.

In keeping with other houses, the sun-baked mud walls were topped with neat rows of thatch and the outside was as white as lime and man's application could make them. There was a chimney to take away the smoke and small glass windows to let in the light. There was a small yard outside, at the front of which stood a pair of neat, well-painted iron gates. They were made by Pierce's Ironworks in Wexford town and it was a visit to an iron-makers that was to be the ultimate act in the life of the farmer in this story, for it was his undoing.

Wheels on farm carts at that time were made of wood with the outer rim surrounded by bands of iron. The farmer decided to travel to Wexford town to get new bands for a pair of wheels that needed attention, along with some other things as well.

He brought a man with him to drive the horse and cart on the journey and to generally make himself useful, and when they arrived at Wexford the farmer left the man in the town to go about his business. What the man did for the day we do not know, we can only surmise that he sat on a high stool in some drinking establishment for at least part of the day because of what happened later on.

We do not know exactly where the farmer went either; he may have gone to the Star Ironworks in the town, who proclaimed themselves to be sole makers of quality wheel rakes, swath turners, hay cars, tumblers, rakes and lots more, or he may have returned to the makers of his gates.

The iron bands took some hours to make and when they were ready the 140-year-old farmer took delivery of them, planning to take them home with him and fit them on the morrow to the farm cart.

It being evening time by now, the farmer began to search for his transport home. If he could find the conveyance tied up somewhere then he knew he would find the driver, no matter what level of sobriety he had been able to maintain. If all else failed, and once he found the cart and the man concerned, he could drive it home himself and take issue with the driver on the morrow when matters might be somewhat more sober.

Nevertheless, he found it impossible to locate cart or driver anywhere in the town of Wexford that evening. After failing to locate him in the likely spots the farmer began to enquire in the pubs and drinking places along the way to see if there had been any sightings of him at all.

It was eventually confirmed that the driver had convinced himself that the farmer had struck out for home without him. Nobody cared to offer an explanation for this strange turn of events, or even tried to fathom the man's reasoning. Accordingly, they said, the driver had made as much haste as he could to follow the departed farmer, who instead of being before him was now left well behind him.

The 140-year-old farmer was by now standing in the street with two large hoops of iron around his shoulders ready to throw up on the cart and away for home – except there was no cart to throw them upon. It was departed and gone, like the snows of last winter.

Throwing reason to the wind, the old man left the town of Wexford in pursuit of his departed driver and his conveyance back to his homestead. Even with two iron bands on his back he set off happy enough that he would overtake the driver and the cart at a pub along the road, for the horse drawing the cart had seen better days and was not as swift as it once had been. Arriving at Taghmon he was sure he had caught up with the errant driver; but soon discovered that the cart and driver he sought were not there. On enquiring after his driver and describing the man he was seeking, the farmer was told he had left the place only a short time earlier. So, he travelled on.

Men of the time were described elsewhere as being low of stature, well set, thick and strong, clear skinned, compact and strong-bodied. Moderation in diet was said to secure them from many distempers and so it was with this farmer; he had never known a day's sickness in his life, leaving aside bad toothache from rotting teeth – none of which were now left in his head to bother him. But healthy or not, we may suppose that hunger, frustration and not a little fatigue was by now affecting the 140-year-old man, who after all was carrying two large hoops of iron on his back which would have been hard work for a man a hundred years his junior.

Arriving at Waddington, by now slower in pace than when he had set out, he was told that his driver and the cart had left there too. He walked on. His gait became shorter and shorter, and his progress slower and slower. He did not catch up with

the driver who, even when he reached his journey's end to discover that his passenger was not home before him, did not turn and trace the road backwards seeking the old man and his bands of iron.

The walking man could have cast his burden aside and stayed somewhere for the night, hiring another cart to take him home with his iron hoops in the morning; but he chose not to do so. That night he walked every step of the road from Wexford town to his own house at Bannow. It was a 20-mile walk for a man who was 140 years of age. It was a distance and a burden that would have challenged a younger man, but he arrived home to his own place in the end with his vexatious and heavy bands of iron along with him and lay down to rest on his bed.

He worked away at his farming tasks in the days that followed but seemed put out to all who knew him. Few were surprised a few days later when he took ill and passed away from the exertion and torment of it all. Other than that, he was healthy enough when he died and it was said that, had it not been for that long walk and the burden he carried in such a trying way, he would have lived longer; but who knows what lies in store for any of us, whether we are aged one year or 140 years.

We never heard tell of what happened to the driver or the horse or the cart. They may be wandering between Wexford and Bannow to this day, or their ghosts might well be, in search of two bands of iron and a farmer determined to sleep in his own bed at the end of the day, come what may.

Eight

PEGGY EDWARDS' RATS

Long ago, people used to wander the roads for all sorts of reasons. Some had no home of their own; some had a home but travelled in the course of business. Some even made it a condition of their work that, when they arrived at the client's home, they be accommodated by the household they worked in for as long as was needed. Some of these people were poor and others were not poor at all.

Every month or so, according to Brigid Ní Eadhra from Fethard, a travelling man named Jim Hughes came around the Templeton area with a horse and van. This was in the mid-1930s when many people in Wexford and across the world were hungry for want of work. But, Jim Hughes was not poor. He sharpened scissors and scythes for people for a living and was never short of work. He charged sixpence and was proud of his craft. People liked him and welcomed him, though he was old and peculiar in his ways.

He had a big dog called Shep that he treated like a human being and one day, when he was sharpening some household items for a woman in her own home, it came to meal time and the dog fell hungry. The woman had already agreed to cook for Hughes but he also asked her to fry a mackerel he had brought for Shep.

Well, so she did, whatever she thought of the imposition of being asked to cook for the tradesman's dog. However, she put the dead fish on the griddle over the open fire and forgot about it as she attended to her other duties. The fish was smoked first, then it was burnt, then it was charred, and by then it was of no use to man or dog. Hughes and his hungry dog left the place but not before he told her that if she could not cook for a dog she could not cook for a Christian.

Hughes was harmless enough. Others of his kind were treated with suspicion and few householders would agree to cook for them. Many were allowed to sleep in the barn but some farmers did not like to let anyone they did not know sleep in their barn, for it was not unknown for one to fall asleep over a lighted pipe and to set fire to the place, sometimes himself included.

Travelling tinsmiths made and sold tea drawers, basins, mugs and cake tins; others made clothes or essential household items. All stayed in a district for just a few days until commerce was exhausted, whereupon they moved on. Many grew tired from walking along winding roads that seemed to go around everything and through nothing; it could take a long time to get anywhere by the roads in the old days.

Why this should be so, was related by Margaret Walsh, a pupil in Ringville National School, who had the explanation from her seventy-six-year-old grandfather Walter Hennebry of Ballinlaw. Whether it is true or not is hard to say. Long ago in Ireland there were very few houses, and not that many people either. Cattle left grazing in the fields would come home every evening to be milked. The first of the cows would make her way across the grass and the others would follow in her track and thus a path was made. When men went out to work they naturally went by the path that the animals had made, and so it grew wide and eventually flat stones were thrown down to make it dry and clean. By and by the fields were divided up and walls and ditches grew up as boundaries; and the twisting road was made the border. Houses were built beside it on both sides, in the fullness of time. A few houses made a village and, by and by, the village grew into a town with more houses and a few shops gathered together. But for years afterwards roads still twisted along the line that was marked by the milch cow hundreds of years before. Where the old cow led, everyone followed.

In those days few people had money to spend and little way of earning any. Instead, they got things by swopping something they had for something else that they needed. People who grew produce or caught fish, or picked cockles or mussels would take them into the town to barter with the shopkeeper for their needs. No money changed hands. It was a common sight to see two or three people walking along with little sacks on their arms full of picked cockles or other shellfish. If they could not make a bargain with a shopkeeper they would call to the various houses on days of abstinence with them, not selling them, but exchanging them for a plate of wheat meal here, some flour there, perhaps a bit of butter or even a packet of tea. Days of abstinence were days when the eating of meat was prohibited by religious belief. Friday was generally such a day, and sales of fish products went up that day and the day before, in readiness.

Peggy Edwards was an old woman who picked cockles all week until Thursday night. She then set off for Ross at midnight to be in the fish house at Ross at 8 a.m. on the following morning, ready to sell her goods – or so folklorist Jim Delaney was told by eighty-four-year-old Patrick Eustace, a local farmer and labourer who lived that way in the 1950s.

It was 16 miles to Ross from Bannow, where Peggy started from. She sold what she could in the market for the best price she could get and whatever was unsold she offered from door-to-door in the town afterwards. In her prosperous years when she was able to get about smartly and when her earning capacity was at its height, she had a little ass and cart to get from one place to another. Work was hard, but at least she did not have to foot every step of the journey carrying her goods on her back.

In her later years she had slowed down, as many had before her. She gathered less and she earned less. Her reserves of cash dwindled. Peggy found that when the ass grew old and died she could not buy another beast to carry her and her goods to market, and she had to walk everywhere herself.

Being slower about travelling, she needed longer on the journey. She would set off on Thursday at noon instead of midnight; but now she stopped in some houses in towns along the way and went on to Ross early the following morning.

She was well known on her usual routes. Children loved to see her coming along the road for she carried sweets and cakes with her for them, as a treat, having no children of her own. She travelled to nearby Waterford to sell her goods, as well. She would go to Ballyhack, cross the water on the boat to Passage and then on to Waterford, a good 6-mile walk from Passage to Waterford on aging feet.

On one awful night of wind and rain, being tired of the journey, she asked for shelter at a little house along the road. It was a house she had passed often enough and the children had been the recipient of her gifts as she given them by over the years. She was welcomed by the woman and her five children who lived there (where the man of the house was we do not know) and they shared with Peggy a small supper of potatoes and mussels, which they had gathered from the nearby waterway.

They chatted and discussed this and that, and the children told Peggy of their lives and she told them a few stories of people she met until they had eaten all the potatoes and the basket of mussels contained only empty shells. It was then time for the household to settle down for the night. But before the children went to bed they spilled all the shells out in a heap on the floor until none were left in the basket. This was a strange thing to do, for people usually threw the shells outside the dwelling house; but Peggy said nothing at all to the people who had extended hospitality to her. She was sure there was a reason for what they did. It was a chore they had undertaken before, she could tell.

One by one the voices from the beds around the little house fell silent. Peggy closed her tired eyes, glad to rest before her long journey on the morrow. Suddenly there was an awful commotion beside the table on which they had eaten their meal. Peggy sat up quickly to see an army of rats making for the shells. Arriving at the heap, the rats dove on them and were among them all night, eating and fighting for space and advantage. Seeing what happened, Peggy realised that the family was so poor that they could not defend against the rats or keep them out of the old house, with its myriad ways of getting in for determined rodents. So, instead they left the shells out for the rats to distract them from biting the sleeping children. The night passed and Peggy took her leave of the family the next morning. She was tired, having been kept awake by the noise of the rats, but there was a lift to her step that had not been there for a long time, for she had decided that, whenever she travelled this road, she would stop and make sure the family had from her whatever she could spare

Such was the way people lived in Ireland in the days long gone, when folk wandered the roads for all sorts of reasons and few had any wealth worth worrying about.

Nine

FOUR WISE BROTHERS

Four brothers once lived in a town called Gotham. They were not the brightest sparks ever seen in Wexford – or anywhere else for that matter. In fact, they were known as the Four Wise Men of Gotham, in a salute to their limited intelligence. Gotham does not exist anymore and its exact location remains a mystery. It may have been swallowed up and covered with sand like Bannow, or it may be that a moving bog went over it, as folklorist Patrick Kennedy speculated when writing in 1870. No one he had spoken to knew where it was. No matter, it is enough that we have the story of what happened to the siblings.

They were cheese makers and were industrious enough to be able to afford a horse to go to market on. One market day, one of them took a big cheese to town to sell it. He was on horse-back, and just as he came to the brow of a steep hill outside the town, the cheese fell off its perch and began to roll down the slope of its own volition, and with a vengeance.

Most people would chase the cheese to catch it, especially as a galloping horse might be expected to outrun a rolling cheese, no matter how fast it was travelling. Yet, this Wise Man had other ideas: he would take another road into town and meet the cheese at the foot of the hill. He put spurs to his horse and was soon in the street at the bottom of the hill. However, he was confounded to discover that the cheese was nowhere to be seen.

He rode up the hill, expecting to either meet the cheese coming down or see it toppled over in the dyke, but it was nowhere. Failing in his quest, the brother returned home hungry and thirsty, with neither the cheese nor the value of it from the market to his credit.

In the end, he was blamed for the loss of the fine cheese by his brothers for so long that he began to believe he might have been in some way at fault for its loss. Stung by the remarks and ingratitude of his brothers, he asked them to state what they would have done in his place.

One of his brothers said he would bring another cheese of the same size, roll it down the hill, and ride after it and see where it would go, and in that way might find the first errant cheese. He would then have a pair of cheeses to sell in the market, he claimed. Another said if it happened to him he would sit at the market-cross till he heard a crier calling out where it was to be got, for it would very likely be some honest person that found it. The final brother said he would pay the crier to make the offer of half of it as a reward to the man that found it and returned it. For half a loaf is better than no bread.

Next market day one of the brothers, though not the first lad who was now relegated to the role of supporter, went to sell another cheese, and he was determined he would be ready if any mischance should happen to him. As luck would have it on the day, just at the very same place, he dropped his cheese.

This time it did not roll far, for it came down in a rutted track. This second Wise Man pulled out his sword, and made a prod at it to lift it up, but the sword was too short. So he rode into the town to the swordsmiths and bought a long sword with a sharp point, and rode back again. Sadly, his cheese was not where he had last seen it; nor halfway down the hill when he went that far in his search; nor at the very bottom of the hill.

He recollected what was said at home and decided to follow his brothers' suggestions. He first sat at the market cross till sunset to see if the honest finder would call out that he had discovered the cheese. Then he paid the crier to call out an offer of half the cheese to any finder as a reward. But it was all to no avail, and the disappointed man returned home empty-handed – and to no great welcome when he got there, for he had neither the cheese nor its value with him, no more than his brother had before him.

The missing cheese and the safest way to transport runaway cheese became a subject for discussion in that family for a long time; but neither cheese ever turned up, nor did anyone make them any wiser as to where the pair of cheeses had gone after they left the Wise Men's custody.

The loss of the cheeses was put behind them and they went on with life much as before. One of their neighbours had a few marriageable daughters and, in time, a match was made between the eldest brother (the loser of the first cheese) and the neighbour's eldest daughter, and a new house was built for the couple at the end of the big lawn that was a little distance from the main house that all four wise men called home.

The evening before the wedding, the bridegroom said he was rather afraid of married life. He had heard of women tyrannising their husbands and beating them within an inch of their lives; if his new wife took a fancy to trounce him in the night, nobody in his family would hear him from the new house, situated where it was.

The brother that was next in age to the bridegroom, that is to say the second eldest brother, said it should be put in the marriage articles that there could not be a stick kept in the house thicker than a grown man's little finger – on the premise that a maddened wife could not kill anyone with such a weapon in her hand.

That notion gave them all great comfort, till a servant-boy pointed out that, if she was inclined for battle it would not be the little kippeen of a stick she'd take up while she had the fire tongs at hand, for a tongs would beat a thin stick any day, in the matter of husband bashing.

All were thrown into a quandary again, but the boy soon gave relief when he suggested a plan of action. It was a pity he had not spoken up in the matter of the missing cheeses and they might still have them or the value of them from the market; but nobody had thought to ask him.

His plan was as follows: if the new mistress, God bless her, decided to whack the young master, he was to bawl out like a man. A stable boy would hear him from the stable loft. He in turn would bawl out, and the thresher would hear him from his heap of sheaves in the barn. The servant boy said he would be the final link in the chain of alert. He would hear the thresher from the settle-bed in the kitchen, where he would be resting. He would tell the mother of the four brothers, and all the house would no doubt hear a wakened mother's opinion of her daughter-in-law.

Needless to say, they all clapped their hands for joy, and the marriage ceased to frighten anyone anymore, and it went ahead. The day was celebrated and the wedding was made, and the first night passed as it should. The unmarried brothers and their pals spent the best part of the night making noise outside the house and blowing through glass bottles with the ends cut out of them to make even more noise; but even the maddest person grows weary and they fell away in time to leave the new couple alone.

Not to be outdone, and to keep to their bargain, the stable boy, the thresher, and the boy in the settle-bed who had started it all said they didn't close an eye for a whole week after the marriage, for fear of an attack on the master. As there had been nothing more than a few good whispers coming from the new house all week, no one stayed awake after that.

That marriage went so well that the remaining three Wise Men of Gotham married the bride's sisters. It meant mighty confusion in the matter of cousins when children were born, as to who was related to who and in what way. Still, even though they all married and moved out of the family home one at a time, they would not live a foot farther apart than the four corners of the big lawn where they all built houses, identical to one another.

Matters progressed so until they were all conversing one day in the open and a remark was made that put them all into a great fright, for it was easy to frighten the Wise Men. Are we not four brothers altogether, one asked the others. They agreed they were, to be sure. They were called the Four Wise Men of Gotham, everyone knew that. Well, the first brother said, he had counted and could not make out one more than three, when his tally was done. All did the calculation and arrived at the same figure of three brothers. They thought one brother must be gone away and it had not been mentioned and they were disturbed and frightened, for a while. At last, the brother who had spoken first said they should all go and sit on the ridge of his house, and they would soon see which brother was missing.

Well, they did so, and then the poor fellow who stayed on the ground to count, after looking all round, cried out, 'There's no one on my own house. It's myself that's missing!' They all came down then to console him and to welcome him home now that they knew he had been missing and was returned.

Such was the way the Four Wise Men of Gotham passed their days. And small harm to them.

Ten

HALF~WITS AND OTHER FOOLS

Most counties in Ireland have their complement of people who are not the full shilling. Indeed, the folklorist and writer Patrick Kennedy came across some of them in the early 1800s in his home county of Wexford and noted them down for us.

One man, who went by the name of Murtheen, was said to not have had an ounce of sense in him. People thought him such a fool that they would not walk on the same side of the road as him, for fear of what he might do; he, for his part, kept as far away from everyone as the road would allow him.

It was said that he went to school for a while and then stopped. While he was there his sole answer to any question of piety or moral error would be the triad of gluttony, envy, and sloth. Which is maybe why people noted his great feeding habits, for it was said that if you set a pot of stirabout before him he would not stop until he had swallowed every lump of it – and licked the spoon clean afterwards. In that, he was very like one Dick Shones Fuar, who believed that a good meal for a full grown man would be a stone of potatoes and a dozen head of herrings. That said, he also believed that whoever went beyond that was no better than a glutton, so a sense of perspective is still to be observed.

Dick came, one evening, to a poor widow woman's cabin in Ballyhighland, while she was straining the water from her little pot of potatoes at the door. She went inside to let down a little falling table for herself and to spread the cloth over it in preparation for the meal. When she came out for the pot there was not a single potato left in it, for Dick had eaten

them, every one. He was by then sitting very comfortably on the little flag seat outside the door while knocking some crumbs from his recent feast off his coat, for he was tidy if he was nothing else.

Another such denizen of the road was Pat Neil, whose vagaries were well known. He carried no bag, never asked for alms, and brought whatever money was given him back to his old father and mother, who lived in Askinvillar, within sight of Mount Leinster. Though a fool and his money are soon parted, Pat considered that half a loaf was better than no bread and he gave the money up to his people. The food he kept to himself, in his belly.

He had his regular stages for food and shelter at the priest's house and among the farmers of the district. His left foot was always enveloped in a mass of cloths, and protected by a stout circular leather. He did not have the sight of his left eye, which some say gave him a slight reputation as an oracle of sorts.

He told stories in return for his food and hospitality, and most of his stories concerned someone they all recognised, or thought they did. He often related the following story of his father's childhood:

A crowd gathered one Sunday behind the alehouse in Courtnacuddy, a few miles from Enniscorthy, to watch a cockfight. When the cursing, swearing, and scolding were at their worst, what did they see but the Devil flying over their heads with a great quake in his back; they saw his fiery eyes and his horns and hoofs quite plainly. Attracted by such sinful behaviour, his fore-claws stretched down to pick up those gathered. Terrified, the crowd scattered as all ran for their lives. The Devil was so confused striving to catch them all at the same time, and so bothered for letting any of them escape, that he dropped Pat's father, whom he'd managed to catch in his first swoop. (Pat said he had heard this from his father so it had to be gospel truth.)

The Devil let out a great curse and darted down after the boy, but the little fellow touched the blessed earth within the chapel-yard first, before the Devil could grab him. The Devil had not noticed that he was flying over sacred ground and made a plunge at the boy, and in his hurry the end of one of his talons struck against something on the consecrated ground. He gave such a spring and roar that every house in the town shook, and the glass was smashed in all the windows. In his anguish, his hind claws caught the thatch of the dram-shop, or drinking house, that had a half-door that looked towards the chapel-yard, and whipped away the whole roof. It immediately caught fire and flew in a blaze through the air till it landed in the old town alongside the little stream that ran to the mill of Dranagh. Six men who were sloping in the tap-room at the time legged it without finishing their drinks, a miracle you might say, and the unbeliever that lived at the back of the chapel said his prayers that evening for the first time in a long while.

And that was how Pat's father escaped from the clutches of the Devil; a lucky escape and the reason why none of the Neils had much truck with cock-fighting, ever since, from that day to the day Pat told the story, and probably up to the present day, if truth be known.

The same collector also came across a number of intercon-nected stories, this time of foolish women, if there could be such a thing.

The first foolish woman had no window to her mud-wall cabin at all, not even a small one without glass, as you might find among the poorer people of the area. The only door was turned to the north, so she was in dire need of sunlight for comfort and illumination. One day when a caller came to the house, he found her running in and out of the only door with a sieve in her hands crying out that she had it now, she had it now. The man watched this activity for a while, with a puzzled cock to his head. He asked her what it was she had that she was making such a fuss and festival about. She explained patiently that she was trying to carry the sunlight of the day into the cabin, but could never get it inside the door before she lost it again.

The caller thought for a minute and then enquired if she had a pickaxe in the house. She did. He asked her for it and when it was brought (with great difficulty) to him, he went to the wall next to the sun. He gave two or three strokes of the pickaxe and soon enough, for no mud wall will withstand a pickaxe for long, a square window had appeared in the wall and a splash of light was on the floor for the first time since the thatcher was done with the roof.

He left her there, that woman with the sieve, inside the house looking out admiring the brightness of the sun on her face where she sat in her sugán.

Not long afterwards, the same man found himself walking by another cabin where such roaring and bawling as would frighten the dying soul was coming out through the door. The closer he came to the door the louder the noise became, until there was no doubt in his mind that the caterwauling was coming from inside the dwelling.

He became alarmed and so ran in, to find a man sitting on a chair with a clean linen sack on his head and shoulders, his wife bringing a beetle down on his head like the hammers of death, and he roaring like fifty bulls all thrown into a ring together. (A beetle is a tool with a heavy head and a handle, used to ram, crush, and drive wedges into reluctant surfaces, as everyone knows well.) While her husband was roaring away from inside the bag she was saying nothing, for she was too taken up with her work to make much noise, for a change.

The caller asked the foolish woman what she thought she was doing and if she wanted to kill the poor man altogether. She replied that she did not, for he was her husband; she wanted to make a hole in the shirt to let his head and face up through it. It was a cheap and easy way to make a working shirt for an ordinary man, but it was of no use if he could not see out of it; it needed to be down around his neck and shoulders to fulfil that purpose.

To rake a fire on the edge of a lake, or to throw stones on a strand, is as foolish as to advise a silly woman on matters of importance, so the caller asked her if she had any scissors about her? She answered that she would be a poor housewife if she did not. She gave the scissors to the caller who used it to make a cut in the top of the bag, whereupon the poor bruised head of her husband emerged from its prison.

For such simple actions are some men called wise among the foolish.

Eleven

Dizzy
Woman

During the eighteenth century and the early part of the nineteenth century, the village of Forth was very remote and no Forthman would venture on the perilous journey to Dublin without very good cause. It was too far and it was too dangerous a journey and, if by chance he did make it there, then the capital city was not at all reassuring for a man from the countryside.

One day, however, a Forthman was bequeathed a legacy. At first all was well as he thought he had to do nothing but await delivery of his inheritance; but he soon discovered that a journey to the capital was necessary before the bequest would become his; that was the condition.

To put the journey in context, in 1777 there were but three post offices in the entire county – at Gorey, Enniscorthy and Wexford. The Royal Mail from Dublin entered the county only two days in the week, and returned on each succeeding day. The mail bags were never allowed to exceed in weight what the post-boy's horse could carry in panniers slung across his withers and behind the saddle. It was usual then for post offices to keep a list of the names of all townlands in their districts, but in the absence of a comprehensive postal delivery system, letters often lay for weeks before reaching the party whose name they bore.

The heir, who lived in a quiet part of Forth, lived when people throughout their lives did not move more than a parish or two away from where they were born. When word came to him on that day that he was the beneficiary of an inheritance it was exciting news indeed, for he did not know that he was related to anyone who would have enough over from living to leave something to another when they were dead. He was a simple man and, though he could deal with banshees, evil spirits and the little people who ran off with his livestock, and though he could defend himself with his stick if he was caught up in a faction fight at a fair, he was quite terrified of the journey to Dublin and what might befall him along the way.

He was given to believe that whatever he was to receive was in the form of money; no property was involved. It meant that he could carry away whatever it was with him. But that also meant that if he was assaulted and robbed, the attackers could make off with his inheritance. Nevertheless, the man wanted to pay respect to his benefactor by personally accepting whatever it was he was due to receive in Dublin, a city so many miles away. So he agreed to the condition.

He went to the local priest and related his fears in the confessional – having first admitted to the sin of avarice, just in case he had exceeded his desire for his impending good fortune. The priest gave him absolution and asked when he was going to Dublin? As soon as possible, was the reply. The priest, however, suggested that he wait until a Monday a month hence to start off on the road to fortune. The Forthman was quite prepared to accept the holy man's advice for, after all, it was his job to know these things. The priest said that he would say masses for him in all local churches to ensure a safe journey and promised they would all be praying for him until he returned safe and well to his own place under the brow of the hill. The man understood that if a donation was forthcoming on his return, then even more masses would be said for him. Sundays came and Sundays went and the man walked as fast as he could between the churches so he could hear himself being prayed for.

Everyone congratulated him and, remembered themselves to him, even the ones he did not know, and wished him well on the journey. The priest even turned up at his house on the following morning in his pony and trap with the soft-minded young lad from down the road driving it.

They took him to the main road where he caught the stage coach to Dublin … and that is where he vanished and the story ended, as far as we can ascertain. For the last time anyone saw him he was waving at the priest and the boy from the carriage window with his borrowed good cap in hand.

He never came back to his own place, nor wrote to anyone, nor sent word by any means as to what transpired when he arrived at the solicitor's office in Dublin, so far away. He may have found himself the owner of a large fortune or a small one, or nothing at all beyond an empty box. Even the priest who made enquiries through ecclesiastical channels could not find out what had happened to him. If he came into a large fortune and went away to America he did so under a different name to the one he had in Forth. If he received little or nothing at all he may have been marooned in the city and perished there. Or, he might just have decided that he preferred the anonymity of city life to the all-knowing all-seeing milieu of a country area where a priest would have umpteen masses said for your safe return with the money.

Travel can be an eye-opening experience for some. For others, it can lead to tragedy or even terror at the unknown. Such terror once visited a good woman from the same county, though in a different place. Tacumshane was a small village located south of Wexford town, in the southeast of County Wexford. At one time, the nearby lake boasted excellent fish and fowl in abundance. The naval officer John Barry, who is often credited as being the father of the American navy, was born in Tacumshane, as a matter of interest, though he had no connection that we know of with the woman in this story.

A number of stories are told of ships lost in Tacumshane. One phantom ship was spotted by a watchman on board the wreck of the *Bayard*, off Carne. He reportedly saw a large ship heading directly for Tacumshane beach. The night was still, with no breeze at all, yet the fully rigged ship continued to hold her course for land, despite the watchman raising blue warning lights on the wreck.

The ghost ship made for another wreck in the same locality, and then seemed to go aground at the rocks, near Carnsore Point. When two local men put out in a small boat and rowed to the spot to see what they could do, there was no trace of any ship.

In 1837, the brig the *Spanish Packet* was wrecked at Tacumshane, and seven of the crew were drowned.

So the area and its inhabitants could hardly be described as insular and unused to the wider world, either from direct experience or by reports from those who had travelled farther afield than others. Yet, the following story comes to us from the early nineteenth century when many Wexford families never crossed the county borders.

An elderly woman, wife to a respectable farmer, came to the local rector, Revd William Eastwood on business. He offered her food, and while she was eating her breakfast, she revealed that she had never been out of Forth, had never been to any market town but Wexford, for that matter.

But, she revealed while she chewed away on her meal, she had been prevailed on one unlucky day to go to the summit of a mountain, which the rector stated afterwards to be about 50m above the level of the surrounding countryside, but which to his informant was very high indeed. Arriving safely at the summit she said she was astonished and overcome at seeing the wide world that opened to her view from the elevated vantage point. However, her head grew giddy and her stomach turned sick, and she returned homewards, fully determined to never again expose her life and senses to such hazards. And nor did she.

Perhaps her county man decided the opposite after his dealings with his local clergyman and decided that the best thing for him to do was to never return to his own parish again. After all, there was a whole world awaiting the man who wanted to expose his life and newfound senses to such hazards.

As for the dizzy woman, she had seen enough to last her a lifetime.

Twelve

THE WOMAN
WHO SWORE

We don't hear all that much nowadays about the Good People, the fairies, swapping one of their children for a human child, but it was a widespread practice at one time in the rural parts of Wexford, according to stories told down through the generations.

According to Patrick Kennedy, one such occurrence was reported in about 1809 from Tobinstown in the pleasant valley of the Duffrey, which was sheltered from the north-west winds by the huge mound of Mount Leinster. Two villages were separated here by a turf bog. The western one was called Kennystown, the eastern, Tobinstown. The Rath of Cromogue commanded the bog to the north, which drained away to the south. On a summer's day, dry tussocks of the bog provided a handy seating place for families on an afternoon.

Katty Clarke of Tobinstown was happy in the possession of a fine boy, the delight of her eyes and heart, till one unlucky day, when she happened to sleep too long in the morning. As a consequence, she had not time to say her morning prayers, whereupon things took a turn for the worst.

Her husband, coming in from early morning work in the fields, was annoyed to find his stirabout was not ready for him. But Katty was as vexed with her man and his demands as she was with herself for slipping up in her daily duties. She soon threw a bowlful of stirabout before her husband and banged about their home for a while, trying to catch up with her work. Her language was strong and brooked no response; she even said a few curses and the odd swearword, though it was hard to tell, so fast was she speaking. Her man thought it best to take himself off out of the house as soon as possible, and so she was left alone with the child.

All these annoyances prevented her from remembering the holy water in its clay font on the wooden frame of the door. It was used to bless those leaving the house so as to keep them safe while they were abroad, until their return. She passed it by on the way out without sprinkling some drops on her little son, and making the sign of the cross on his innocent forehead, as she usually did.

When the men and boys left the yard for their outdoor work Katty took a pailful of dirty linen to the spot where the stream formed a little pool, and where the villagers had set a broad and flat beetling stone to beat the dirt out of soiled clothing. While she was employed in cleaning the clothes as best she could, she let her child roll about on the grassy slope behind her, as was her wont.

All went well enough with the arduous work and some of her annoyance at her morning fallibility was spent on the innocent clothes under her command, when all of a sudden she heard a scream from the boy. Maternal instincts ablaze, she turned from her task and ran to him. She found her son to be in convulsions on the ground where she had lain him just a short while ago, safe and sound. His body was twitching and his head was

thrashing from one side to another. His face was contorted and his tongue seemed to want to leave his mouth; blood escaped from the corner of his twisted lips where his teeth had closed on his tongue, drawing blood. His distorted face was dreadful to see for anyone, but more so for his concerned mother.

She held on to him and tried to calm him with her country woman's strength, but could not do so. When he calmed a little of his own accord, she picked him up and ran home to her little house where she had lately had words with her husband about stirabout and delayed breakfast. It all seemed so long ago, now.

Once in the door, she placed the semi-lifeless form of her son on the bed and administered salt and water and other remedies that were popular in such country parts long ago. The fit passed and the boy fell into a restless sleep, but she was grieved to see that the wizened, pained expression still remained on his face, and that his whimpering and whining did not abate. In the days that followed, crying was never far from his mouth.

The boy woke eventually and seemed to be himself, though with an old shriven face on him and a hunger that a ploughman could not beat. He ate as much as would suffice a full-grown man and was always ready for food both at meal-times and any time at all.

Her husband had fallen quiet when he saw their son, for he knew that his wife was a good mother and whatever had happened had been out of her control. It was not anything she had failed to do, he assured her. Even the crawthumper that lived in the next field assured her that the absence of holy water on his forehead for one morning was not the cause of his torment; for God looks after his own innocents, she said – though she added a special prayer at rosary for his intentions in the face of what had happened.

As was the way in the country at that time, neighbours gathered together to address the problem. Everyone was there, from the oldest to the youngest adult in the place. Curious children were chased away from the door but crept back and listened anyway, in a scrum of bodies, through a crack in the weathered door frame.

After a lot of discussion and much examination of the growing boy with the old man's face, the neighbours came to the conclusion that it was a *síogaí* that Katty was now slaving her life out for: a changeling, in other words, swapped by the Good People, the fairies. They had exchanged an ageing one of their own for Katty Clarke's fine boy.

Katty's extended family came to the same persuasion, so too did her husband, though he kept his own counsel, and eventually, but with some doubts, Katty began to believe it herself.

What followed next was a well-rehearsed ritual around the country where such happenings occurred. If the Good People were able to discommode the way of humans, then humans would look to retrieve their own with an alacrity and skill handed down to them through folklore and custom.

The family and neighbours gathered around the fire in the house where the *sighe* slept. A neighbour, a friend of the man of the house, took a shovel, rubbed it clean and laid it on the floor, and his wife, the mother of eight children of her own and two grandchildren by then, seized on the young form. She placed it sitting on the broad iron blade. She held it there stoutly, notwithstanding its howls, while her husband, raising the shovel gently, proceeded to the bawn that surrounded the homestead. He was accompanied by the assembly, and, despite all opposition on the part of the *sighe*, it was placed on a wisp of straw that crowned the manure heap. The luxury of the setting did not succeed in arresting its outcries, said people who were there; but his audience, not taking much notice, joined hands and in the native Irish tongue, the voice of the generations that went before, serenaded the crowned heap three times, while the fairyman, who had been summoned for the occasion, recited an incantation, known to everyone there as sure they knew their own and their family name.

He called on the mother of the *sighe* to come and remove her offspring, for food and drink he had received and kindness from the woman of the house. The *síogaí* could no longer stay but must depart whence he came. That much declared, the offer was made that if the lost child was restored, food would be left for the Good People. It would be left when the cloth was spread on the harvest-field, on short grass newly mown; food would be left on the dresser-shelf, and the hearthstone would be clean when the fairy host came to sweep in rings round the floor to feast before the fire. He ended by calling once more for the mother of the *sighe* to restore the mortal child, and to receive her own in return.

This was repeated three times and when it ended, all concerned left the *sighe* where it lay, re-entered the house, and closed the door to await a response. It was not long coming. The people soon felt the air around them sweep this way and that, as if it was stirred by the motion of wings, but they remained quiet and silent for about ten minutes (some claimed it was only ten seconds but that's humans for you; they can agree on little that matters). When all was still once more, they opened the door, the better to look out, and saw the straw on the manure heap, but neither child nor fairy was to be seen anywhere.

The fairyman ordered Katty to go into her bedroom to see if anything was left on the bed for her. She did so, closing the door behind her. All was silent, all waited; the only sound was the tumbling of a half-burnt sod of turf in the fireplace. Then they heard a cry of joy and Katty was among them in a moment, kissing and hugging her own healthy-looking child, who was waking and rubbing his eyes, and wondering at the lights and all the eager faces of people around him. Men were slapping one another's backs; women were queuing up to kiss the baby and the children, who by now had infiltrated the room, were leaping about the place like spring lambs gone mad.

In the end all left the little family alone and went to their homes. Katty and her husband lay down in their own bed with their newly restored son between them.

From then on, whatever hurry Katty might be in of a morning, neither she nor her husband ever left their bedside till they had finished, as devoutly as they could, five Paters and five Aves, and an Apostles' Creed and a Confiteor. Nor did they leave the house without a sprinkling of holy water. And Katty never cursed or swore at her husband beneath her breath except when she was surprised by a sudden fit of passion, which is a different matter and story altogether.

Thirteen

MONEY FOR NOTHING

Some people don't want to lift a finger for themselves – but they are happy for others to give them money for doing nothing. These are the type of people who will search the roads in the morning, or at evening time, to find a lurechan, or similar, who can, willingly or unwillingly, tell them where they might find some gold that they can have for their own use, without any further effort. They would rather do this than go to work, though truth to tell, there is a great deal of effort involved in finding a lurechan and persuading him to hand over the gold. Work might come easier.

There are numerous sightings of lurechans in Wexford County, though no more than there are in other parts of the country, for fairies everywhere all need their feet shod for parties or pranks alike and it is the lurechan who has the job of doing that. But the lurechans of Wexford seem to be a canny lot. There are very few, if any, reports that a lurechan was bested by a human in the matter of handing over the little man's trove of gold. Lurechans are also called leprechauns by some people; but no matter what they are called they will not give up their gold easily.

The lurechan is mostly found in shady nooks or beside a tumbling stream where not too many people pass by. It is not usual to find a pair of lurechans working together at making shoes for they are solitary beings. And if he is not talking to someone then he is thinking his own thoughts and hammering away at the shoes before him for others to wear.

His own clothes have been described as a red square-cut coat, richly laced with gold, a waistcoat of the same, a cocked hat, shoes and buckles. Others say he wears a green jacket and a long, pointed red cap; the difference may be in personal choice, or even the district that he frequents, for tradition is all when you are dealing with a small man that only comes up to the waist of a fully grown human.

It is well known that the small cobbler has the power of deception, to an extraordinary degree. He uses this power to deceive his antagonists from the world of man when they seek to take from him that which is his own. No man has been recorded with any degree of accuracy as having bested a lurechan in an encounter of wits.

Ghosts and fairies were far more common a hundred years or more ago than they are now, according to Martin Grady, a labourer from the Carrick-on-Barrow area, who in 1937 recalled for Mícheál Mac Aodha that there was a young man who lived in Rathimny, in the parish of Tintern, who was going across a field one day and he saw a lurechan.

The labourer was a fine active young man, so he made a run at the lurechan and caught him. And although the small fellow turned and twisted this way and that way, the swift lad succeeded in holding him till the struggle eased. 'If you tell me where there's money hid, I'll let you go', said the captor, but the lurechan said nothing. He began to twist and turn again, trying to get away.

A lurechan possesses the power of bestowing unbounded wealth on whoever can keep him within sight until be is weary of the surveillance and gives the ransom demanded. These are the rules of engagement: the mortal fortunate enough to surprise one and seize him must never withdraw his gaze from him until the threat of destruction forces the lurechan to produce the treasure: turning away loses contact and the reward.

The young man said, 'It is well known that you know lots of secrets about money that is hidden and unless you tell me where the money is to be found I will sweep off your head with my knife' and produced the said weapon from his pocket.

Realising that he was caught, the lurechan said there was money hidden in the middle of the field they were standing on. The way he would know it from any other, if he came back, was that there was a single boochalawn, or ragwort, growing over it.

Taking a chance, the young man looked around the field, which was well cared for by its owner. There wasn't a weed to be seen except for one big boochalawn in the middle. Ragwort is generally to be found in a field that has been overgrazed; but there was just a single, yellow-topped ragwort standing in this field.

The young man was delighted with himself and he let go the lurechan who vanished in a second, as you might expect. It was like he had never been there. The young man went home for the night and arose on the following morning as soon as daylight came in to his bedroom.

Out of the bothán at the back of the house he took out a spade and a pickaxe, and set out for the field of the single boochalawn. But when he got there he couldn't believe his eyes, for every inch of the field was covered with yellow-topped waving boochalawns.

Try as he might, he could not find which had been the single ragwort the previous day – he had been bested by the Lurechan.

Thomas Murphy of Portersgate reported a similar experience. He knew a man, he said, who caught a lurechan and the captive agreed to show him where a pot of gold was buried.

He did so, telling the man to shove a sharp stick down into the ground until he met resistance. Then he vanished like his predecessor had done, once the man's mind was distracted.

Not to be fooled, the man shoved the stick well down until he hit something solid below the surface of the earth. Being unable to do any more with only a stick for excavation, he hurried off home to fetch a pick and a shovel. But when he returned he found, to his astonishment, that the

lurechan had driven 160 additional sticks into the ground. Every one was the identical twin of the original stick. Try as he might, the man could not find the one he wanted, and the lurechan was nowhere to be seen, needless to say. Another human bested.

Another foolish man once met a lurechan and said good morning to him, all the while wondering how he might get close enough to grab him and stare into his eyes. The lurechan, seeing the man was preparing to pounce, remarked to him that he was on the road early, just as early as the man on the other side of the road. Of course, the mortal looked away to see who was across the road, but there was nobody there. When he looked back the lurechan was gone the way of all lurechans. He had vanished.

In spite of all these reports and salutary tales, humans are still being fooled by the quick wit of their quarry. Sometimes, a woman might have a better chance of success than a man might; but not much.

Many years ago, an old woman lived on her own in a small cabin on waste ground at Fethard on Sea, according to Thomas Murphy of Portersgate, whose account of the following manifestation is to be found in the Irish Folklore Commission Collection. One day, she planted some apple trees on the waste ground and they grew and produced bountiful fruit, which she sold to make a living.

In those days, people did not have watches or clocks or calendars to live by; they told the time by the sky and the stars, and life moved along to a different rhythm.

It was the old woman's habit to go to market early, and to get her stock there she carried the apples in a basket on the back of a donkey. On the day this story happened it was autumn and she started out early, for an apple is a nice thing to have of an autumn day and trade was likely to be brisk in the market. Arriving at the foot of a knoll, she heard the sound of tapping and slowed her progress. She saw, to her surprise, a little man sitting on a big stone. He had on a green jacket and a long, pointed red cap. He was repairing old shoes, but the shoes were small. A man's large thumb would probably have filled most of the one under scrutiny.

The woman stopped and stared in amazement. She saw that he was busy and that there were a lot of shoes for him to work on and deduced, therefore, that he must be rich from all the coins the owners of the shoes would give him.

She left the donkey with its burden of apples and stole up behind the lurechan. She moved swiftly, grabbed him by the neck and shouted that he was to make her rich or she would break his neck.

When the usual stratagems failed to work with the apple woman for the lurechan he agreed to show her where the gold could be found; but she would have to take him with her to get to it. That was the condition.

Being a trader of long standing and someone who had heard more than a few stories about the wiles of the Good People and the lurechan in particular, the woman placed her captive on top of the basket of apples and tied him securely to the basket with long cord. She started off on their journey to gold and an easier life. Good progress was made along the road, but shortly afterwards she looked back to see that all was well. She saw, to her horror, that the basket was empty of apples and, what was worse, they were strung all along the road they had just travelled.

'I will have your life', she shouted at the lurechan in her anger and frustration at what he had done, even though he was still tied to the basket. 'Well', said the lurechan, 'release me and I'll hold the donkey so that he doesn't run away while you pick up the apples'.

She untied the lurechan, handed him the reins of the donkey and went back and picked up all the apples, one by one so they did not get any more bruised than they were already. When she turned back all she could see was the donkey grazing; the lurechan, like his companions before, was gone. The woman packed up the apples on the donkey and went on her way.

Not only was no richer in the matter of gold, but the apples were bruised now and would fetch a lower price at market than if they had never bounced off the road behind the slow-moving donkey. She was no better off; instead she was all the poorer for attempting to best the wiliest being in Wexford, the local lurechan.

Fourteen

Treasures
of Wexford

That there is buried treasure all over Wexford County has never been in any doubt. There are few parishes that do not have a true tale of riches lying beneath the soil, to be had by the right person, at the right time, approaching the matter in the correct way. However, finding it and making it your own is a different matter, for traps and obstacles are in place to protect the treasure until its original owner returns to claim it.

Sometimes it is a Norman marauder who hid his plunder until he could return, like a jay bird burying an acorn for when he would next need food; but he may have forgotten where he buried his store or been killed while he was away.

Consider this: in the second field from the house of Patrick Purcell, in Drumdowney, there is a deep hole in which there is a large stone. Patrick's mother recalled that long ago a man called John had a castle near that field. The castle was called Castle John. It was said that he buried his money in a box in that hole. The box was still under the stone in the 1930s, when Patrick related the story in the seventy-ninth year of his life. Frustratingly, the box of money is buried down so deep that it cannot be reached, so there it lies, according to local folklore. At least there are no reports of strange beings on hand to chase people away until John returns, in some form or another, to attend to business.

In Carriganurra, which is situated near the main road from Ross to Waterford, it is said at one time there was a woman living there whose name was Nurra. She had a great deal of money and in a time of trouble she hid it in the ground, away from her home, in case anyone came calling with greedy purpose. There, for some reason now lost to time, the money stayed, never to be recovered by the owner. It is a common belief in the area that the money is there to be found by those who would look properly for it. Several attempted to get to it but none of them succeeded. They tried in droves and in small intense groups, and they tried alone. Richard Kneefe of Ringville was said to be one of those who tried. He was named by local girl Margaret Kearney's grandmother, then aged about eighty-six, as being one of those who returned empty-handed from the task.

Moses Curtis aged fifty-five years from Gusserane, New Ross, recalled a slightly different story from the 1920s when farm worker Pat Walsh was out ploughing the land with a pair of horses. (It was not to be until the 1940s when the first Fordson tractors would begin to replace working horses on farms.) A decent-sized farm in Wexford in the early part of the twentieth century would have used up to eight pairs of working horses to work the land, and on this day Pat was using his favourite pair when a large stone was struck by the plough. The well-trained horses stood stock still and would go no further. Pat, seeing what had happened, unyoked the pair and tied them to a ditch to rest and calm while he investigated the stone, which had lain buried and was now revealed.

He took a long bar of iron and began to tip the stone, digging around and underneath it so that he could see how he might get a chain on it to pull it from the soil and clear the land for better tillage. But Pat himself became rooted to the spot when he finally managed to pull up the stone. For underneath it, so the story goes, was a crock of gold sovereigns, left there by someone so long ago that nobody even knew the secret of their existence.

What happened next is still spoken of in the parish. People in those days did not work by the clock. However, it was usual for people to turn in for regular meals. Pat's fellow workers gathered for their lunch, but when Pat failed to show up they asked themselves where he could be and why he was not coming in for his food. It was well known that an empty sack will not stand and a hungry man cannot give of his best in the field. Some feared he had suffered an accident or met with misfortune. When more time passed, they went looking for him and his horses.

They found the horses right enough but Pat was gone, never to be seen again. The crock (now empty) was still in the hole in the ground where Pat had first uncovered it in the disturbed soil. A single gold coin was found in the green grass not far away, where Pat had dropped it in his haste to be away with his new fortune.

There was nothing to be done but to untie the pair of horses and bring them back to the stables for a new ploughman to take care of them. The pair went willingly enough, for it was all the same to them who they worked with and gold was of no interest to horses.

The next anyone heard of Pat Walsh was the news, or rumour more likely, that he was sailing for America and a new life there. What was certain was that the missing ploughman was never seen again in Wexford, or in Ireland for that matter. There are some who say he died in America shortly afterwards, but since he did not send word on how he was doing, he may well have bought up half the prairie and ploughed away to his heart's content. For that matter, he may never have looked at a plough-horse's behind ever again. He was away with the found gold, one of the few who ever achieved that feat. Or, at least one of the few that we know about, for if he had not vanished out of a Wexford field on a working day no heed might have been paid to his leaving the place.

As far as anyone knows, Pat Walsh was left with no ill effects to his health, unlike a man in Templeton who had his face changed forever when he went seeking gold. Fifty-year-old

John Lambert recalled some eighty years or so ago the tale of a man who dreamt for three nights in a row of a can that held gold, which was buried near Loftus Hall gates.

It is easy to dream of something that you desire and he had often dreamt of this and that; but the man determined to follow this new dream to the hidden treasure. He did not expect there would be a large fortune awaiting him; but he had seen a can with gold in it, and that's the type of dream that is very hard to ignore.

One night, therefore, he arrived on his own at the gates and, going on his hands and knees, he searched the grass beneath him, sniffing about almost like a hunting dog. In the darkness he spotted a hollow with a bar across it. Below that he could see the can with an iron bar across it, protecting it. He leant down to get his scrawny fingers in around the bar and was almost there when a blast of air hit him in the face. He rolled away from the hollow and staggered off home. His face was never the same afterwards. It had been twisted in the blast and he was forever afterwards like a gargoyle in appearance. Still, no matter how many asked him, or how they cajoled him, he would never reveal the resting place of his can of gold. It was for him to know and for them to find, he said with a laugh that sounded a little insane to those who had known him since he was young.

Big houses and castles seemed to be the logical place for buried treasure, the odd field notwithstanding. Mrs Elizabeth Cusack of Lewistown, Duncannon, said one time that there was rumoured to be treasure buried underneath a flag at Kileske Castle.

One night, a crowd of men went there to find the treasure and to divide it up, in equal shares, among them. They brought with them holy water and a ball of wool to guard against non-mortal beings. This was common practice among treasure hunters.

They found the flag readily enough and dug down beneath it. With an effort they raised it up and quickly dipped the wool in the holy water and draped it around the flag. Inside the cordon of holy water it was safe enough to work, for they were under divine protection.

Having achieved the raising of the flag they anticipated an end to their temporal concerns. Instead, they heard a terrible roaring and jangling of chains. When they looked around they saw an enormous bull gouging the earth, on its way to charging them. Well, the men did not wait but scattered in all directions, cascading over the boundary of holy wool as if it never existed and away they went in all directions.

The next morning, it was discovered that the flag had fallen back into its place once more; by whose hand they could not say. Nor did anyone know who owned a bull so ferocious that it would attack a gang of men in the dark of a castle at night.

It is said in many places that when treasure was buried an animal was often killed and buried with it, to guard it until the owner returned. Perhaps there is more to the Greek mythological legend of the golden apples of the Hesperides being guarded by a dragon or serpent than we know, or care to acknowledge.

For it is all very well to be sceptical of such things in company in a brightly lit room. It is a different matter entirely to place your trust and well being in a ball of holy wool in darkness when beasts roar, the earth trembles and all about you have run away.

Fifteen

GRAVE
HAPPENINGS

In some parts of Wexford it was customary for a body to be brought to a cemetery in a coffin all right and proper, but when the graveside was reached, the body, wrapped in a death shroud, was removed from the coffin and placed on the ground. The face was uncovered for a moment so the mourners might take a last look at the late lamented departed, and ensure it was the right person they were burying. The grave was lined with long sods of grass and the body was laid on this. The sides of the grave were also lined with green sods.

The coffin was left sitting on the ground for the use of the first poor person who might require it and who wished to take it away. It was apparently a common enough way of putting the deceased below ground in that area, in the nineteenth century.

Something else that was common in the county during that time was body snatching. Walter Furlong, a farmer of Corrigeen

Grange related the following story to folklorist James Delaney for the Irish Folklore Commission Collection in the 1950s.

A man named Auld Jim who lived in Taghmon once 'rose a body' for a farmer identified only as Paudeen. The farmer and his various accomplices used to sell bodies to doctors for study. This night, the farmer called Jim out of bed at midnight to do a little job for him. It concerned a young lady that had been buried that day, he whispered. The farmer wanted her risen that night. Jim said no. He believed the deceased would haunt him all the days of his life if he disturbed her last resting place. Paudeen urged Jim not to be a coward and promised he would give him five bob for the night's work and a good drink of whiskey along with it. Between hopping and trotting, Jim agreed to undertake the task.

As instructed, he went to the stable, placed the tackle on the grey mare and put the dray car on her to transport the risen body. He found two crowbars and put them in the car because the young woman was buried in a box tomb and crowbars would be needed to lift the top stone off it, to slip the body out without damaging it.

At that time, you could get five years in jail for body snatching, without the option of a fine at all, so Jim needed an extra drop of liquid courage before starting out with the farmer.

After a short journey, they brought the mare and dray car into the churchyard, so she would not be detected on the road by a passer-by – though there would be few enough of them in the early hours of a country morning. They tied her in a corner of the churchyard and set about their business.

They went to the tomb and lifted the top cover with the two crowbars. They lifted up the cover about a foot high and halted. If they lifted it high enough to pull out the coffin, they'd have to lift the lid off altogether and they would not be able to put it back again. So Jim told Paudeen to get a stick to prop it up to the required height.

But a stick could not be depended on to hold the weight; so Paudeen wedged the crowbar on one side of the cover to make an opening just wide enough to get out the coffin. Jim slipped into the tomb and wedged a foot at each side of the long box to lift it up. He was, at that time, a fine strong man and it was no trouble to him, even though he was nicknamed Auld Jim.

But were ifs and ands pots and pans, there would be small work for the tinsmith, for the plan had been to raise the body, drive off with it and collect payment before anyone knew it was gone. All very fine – if nobody else had thought of that too.

At the same time as Jim was lifting the coffin from its resting place they heard the latch on the churchyard gate being lifted. It was about four o'clock in the morning by now and few people would be arriving for first mass yet, before the cock in the henhouse had even stirred his feathers to crow.

Paudeen panicked, let go of the bar he was using to prop the lid up with and took to his heels. The cover of the tomb flopped back into its place with a thud and there Jim was, left with the coffin inside the black vault, in darkness. Being below ground he had not heard the latch of the gate being lifted and did not know why Paudeen had fled.

Jim blessed himself, as well he might, and prayed that the Devil might break Paudeen's neck for he, Jim, would soon be dead along with the young woman in whose grave he presently rested, for no one would ever come to lift the lid off again and he would wither away.

But many minds, great or small, think alike for the intruders in the churchyard were another crowd come on the same mission of resurrection and recompense.

Jim heard footsteps approach the grave and a voice remark that someone had been there already, for there was a crowbar on the ground. They said if they were quick they would get away with the body before the others.

So, they lifted up the cover of the tomb. There were three or four of them and they were able to lift it quickly and in concert. Jim, anticipating being uncovered, took off his coat and wound it round his head. When the intruders lifted off the cover of the tomb Jim jumped up with the coat around his head and let a most unearthly yell out at the men.

They took to their heels and fled, helter-skelter, in all directions for they thought it was the corpse escaping of its own volition. All disappeared in a flash of flailing legs and sobbing breath with contrition in their souls.

Not to show a loss on his efforts or to allow the other crowd to regroup and return on a recce, Jim got his legs around the coffin and, in his renewed state of exultation, lifted it clean out of the grave.

He went over to the corner of the churchyard and brought down the little grey mare and dray car that Paudeen had neglected to untie in his haste to be off. Jim heaved the coffin onto it and set the mare out on the road for home. He climbed onto the car and sat down on the resurrected coffin. And away he went with as much haste as he could summon from the mare. With the speed he attained he could hear the dead girl rattling around inside the coffin. No matter, he lashed the mare with a switch he had for the purpose, all the way to its owner's yard.

It wasn't long till they arrived, all three of them, in Paudeen's yard. Believe it or not, Paudeen was asleep in his bed by this time, hoping to dream the night away, no doubt. Jim shouted at the cowardly rogue to get up. He said he wanted a five-pound note now that he had the corpse in the yard for him. But Paudeen said it was five shillings that was the bargain. Jim replied that he would go to the authorities straightaway and have the lying farmer transported, if he did not hand over the money.

Paudeen rightly pointed out that it was Jim who had stolen the corpse and not him. Jim enquired as to who employed him; whose mare and car had he used; whose crowbar was used to prise open the tomb; and whose same crowbar was lying wherever the other crowd had thrown it away in the dark on their way out of Hades?

Paudeen employed him and then ran away like a cowardly hangman, leaving him there to die. In fact, he said, recalling his prayer in the darkness of the tomb, he could be dead by now only that St Aidan the patron saint of Wexford himself had saved him. This made Jim feel better and, getting no good out of Paudeen, he went across the yard and got up into the car again, and sat upon the coffin with determination in his frame. Paudeen asked where he was going now, in the last few hours before dawn?

Jim said he was going to the authorities with the coffin, and Paudeen would be in the body of the jail before nine o'clock in the morning. Well, Paudeen asked him to come back and promised he would give over the five-pound note and matters would thus be settled between them.

True to his word, Paudeen brought Jim into the house and gave him a five-pound note and a good tot of whiskey. Then they carried the girl indoors and put her coffin in a little scullery at the back of the house, in case anyone should chance by and wonder why there was a coffin sitting on the dray car in the middle of Paudeen's yard whilst he and Jim were hale and hearty and exchanging words over a sup in the house.

Jim eventually unyoked the mare and put her in the stable, and rolled up the five-pound note and put it in his waistcoat pocket. He said a few prayers for the young woman's soul and went to bed, then slept like a thrush till morning came. The body was delivered to the doctor and that was the end of that.

That was the first body that Jim ever snatched; it was also the last. Jim died in or around the year 1914 when he was aged eighty years or so and no longer the strong man he was when he went grave robbing. He told this story to Walter Furlong himself, according to Walter, so it must be true.

Sixteen

THE HELL
OF DRINK

Death is not always a permanent state of affairs in County Wexford. Two men of different times, but both with an association with the village of Oulart in the county, came back from the dead and resumed their lives among the living as best they could manage; though conversation was bound to be strained with those who had to get used to the reality of the living corpse in front of them.

The first case was recounted by Walter Furlong, a Rathnure farmer to Jim Delaney the folklorist in the mid-1950s, more than a hundred years after the event occurred.

Ballinaclash-man Ned Murphy was stricken with cholera in hard times in the mid-1800s. A pandemic had crossed the country and many fell victim to violent diarrhoea and vomiting, which led to death for those who could not be helped in time. Ned was taken to Oulart, where there was a fever hospital, to see if anything could be done to save him. The fever hospital and dispensary at Oulart was established in 1827. It was under the care of a physician, who also acted as apothecary, and who had a residence rent-free, with a salary of £100 per annum.

It is rare enough nowadays to hear of a misdiagnosis of death – you're either dead or you are not – but stories abound from earlier times of people being declared dead when they were in fact only sleeping. Some had fainted, it was said, and only come round when grave robbers took a knife to their fingers to remove valuable rings for resale. Such a misdiagnosis seems to have been made of Ned, for he was declared expired of cholera in the fever hospital itself and his body was moved to the dead house outside.

A dead house was a structure used in olden times for the temporary storage of human corpses before local burial, or until transportation to a distant cemetery was arranged.

When people died in such circumstances, word was sent to relatives or friends to come and collect the body or to make arrangements for its disposal, but Ned does not seem to have had any kin or colleague that could make the journey to Oulart and return with the body. As a result, his former employer, Mr Moran of Blackwater, was asked to attend to the relict of his late employee.

Moran set off about his sad task and in due course arrived at Oulart fever hospital, where he prepared to do his duty by his former worker.

The dead were garbed at the time in a habit or shroud with no back worth talking about in the garment. So, we can only imagine Mr Moran's surprise to find Ned Murphy standing at the door of the dead house in his shroud, holding the backside closed while awaiting the arrival of his benefactor.

It seems he was well enough recovered from the worst excesses of cholera to be able to converse with Mr Moran on his adventures since he was last seen. Ned informed Mr Moran that he had been dead, right enough – in this he said the physician was quite correct in his diagnosis – but he had come back to life again. Not only that, but he was quite prepared to share his experience with anyone that would listen.

Ned said that he had visited Heaven and Hell, while he was lifeless. He did not say whether he walked there or rode on a winged horse; no details at all were furnished of the mode of transport. He did not have a lot to say about Heaven, which was unsurprising, for few who see it return to tell the tale. Or, if they do, they stay quiet in case there is a rush on the place.

On the other hand, he said Hell was a large place with big iron gates. While he did not enter in himself, not wishing to take up residence there, or be noticed, he did have a good long look through the bars of the iron gates at what was going on inside. More importantly, he claimed he recognised a few familiar faces there who had lately departed this present life. For behind the gates, Ned said, were two old ladies chained up inside because of their depredations in drink. Ned, now the expert on the next life, declared that a person would not go to Hell for anything except drink. No.

Mr Moran, who we can only surmise was confounded with the detail of the next world he was hearing from the man he had come to bury, was pleased in a way to hear that people were being brought to book in the matter of over-indulgence in alcohol. Mr Moran was a teetotaller and felt justified in himself to hear of this state of affairs, while having the charity to feel sorry for the souls involved, the poor wretches.

Ned was fond of a drink himself and his vision of Hell did not cure him, for in his succeeding days he carried on with the life of a drinker. No doubt there were some who questioned the veracity of his recollections given all he had been through. But Mr Moran seems to have been happy enough with the outcome of the journey and Ned's observations.

The fever hospital was still in use up to 1911. It was located next to the doctor's residence at Kilnamanagh, and the ruins of the hospital could be identified until recently. It is said locally that the last person to be treated was a nurse, who had worked in the hospital, and she died there in 1911. The hospital closed down a few years later.

It would have closed down around the time that an Oulart man called Ped or Peter Bolger from Raheenaskeagh was being prayed for in the local church, according to local historian Kathleen O'Reilly-Hyland.

Ped was employed on the ill-fated *Lusitania* when it was torpedoed by a German submarine off the Old Head of Kinsale in 1915, with 1,201 souls lost. Miraculously, some 761 people survived the sinking ship, which was en route to Britain from the United States. Word of the sinking soon came to Oulart. It was known that Ped was a sailor aboard the ship and when no immediate word came of his survival, the village went into mourning.

The ship was sunk on 7 May 1915, which was a Friday, and on the following Sunday at Mass in Oulart, Fr Maher, the local priest, prayed for the repose of Ped's soul. All agreed that Ped was a fine man who had perished tragically, yet honourably. They prayed and waited to see if the body would be recovered from the sea, in due course.

However, a week later the family received a telegram that caused consternation and joy in equal measure. It said Ped was not dead at all; but was in fact recovering in hospital in Cork.

The story of his survival, when it emerged from the lips of the formerly dead man, was astonishing. It appeared that when he found himself off the coast of Kinsale in the cold water he clung on to a floating beer barrel as the ship went down. He said it kept him above the water until he was rescued, in an exhausted condition, and taken to hospital in Cork.

Ped returned home safe and well after a while, and lived for many years afterwards in the townland of Killisk. He did not marry or produce offspring, it seems, and instead went to work on a farm with an aunt and uncle who had no children and who left the place to him. He in turn left it to a niece of his when he finally departed life in Oulart in the mid-twentieth century.

We don't know when Ned Murphy died for the second time; but we can only wonder at what his description of Heaven might be like, if he got there, assuming he had subsequently tempered his intake of strong drink. We can but pray that he did not re-make the acquaintance of the two women he calumniated in chains in Hell.

For strong drink is a strange and a wonderful thing at times.

Seventeen

SEEING
THE DEAD

Long ago, Jack Whitty, his brother and another man were on Burrow Strand supplementing their income by gathering up anything the tide brought in for salvage experts to claim, when they saw there were large casks of tallow coming in from the sea. Tallow was a hard fat derived from parts of the bodies of cattle, sheep or horses, and used to make candles, leather dressing, soap or lubricants in the days before mass manufacturing took over from the local artisan.

Jack and the others watched as casks came in whole on the waves, bobbing here and bobbing there, disappearing and then reappearing in the swell. The ones that reached the shore more or less intact were rolled away from the water's edge to be sold to the highest bidder. Others broke open and released their tapered wooden staves to spread tallow across the water.

The men were doing well enough gathering up whatever the tide brought in to them, for they had done this before. They

were all on an equal share of the profits and all were as determined as the next man to extract as much income as possible
out of the day's work. When they had amassed a decent pile of
salvaged material, Jack's brother went off to bring the jennet
(the offspring of a stallion and a female donkey) and cart onto
the strand to take the salvage away.

There was a tradition in some parts of Wexford that when
an empty boat came ashore after a drowning, the boat was left
where it touched land, as a memorial to the lost souls that were
in it. But there was no boat on the strand this day; there was
just flotsam and debris from the sinking. While waiting for the
others to return, Jack looked along the water's edge to see if
anything more of value was come ashore.

He was startled to see what appeared to be the form of a man
lying at the water's edge a little way off from where he stood. It is
not a sight you expect to see in a normal day's work, but the sea
can release its grip on bodies at any time and so it now appeared.
He went to see if the man was alive but the sailor was beyond
rescue; life was gone out of his body; he would sail no more.

Jack was afraid to touch the body. He could see that no
amount of effort on his part would retrieve its departed soul.
He went to wait beside the mound of tallow for the others to
return. He sat and tried to calm his breathing, staring out to
sea and deliberately avoiding the spot where the body lay. But
try as he might he could not keep his eyes from straying back
towards the corpse; only this time, his view of the body was
obscured by the form of someone sitting beside him.

For the moment he thought it was one of his companions
taking a rest on the pile of barrels and half-barrels and other
gear. But, then his own heart nearly ceased beating as he realised it was the dead man sitting beside him. He too was staring
out to sea, as if waiting for his companions to join him in
silence on the strand.

Jack did not wait for his friend or his brother to come up to him; he took to his heels and ran away. When he was a distance away he looked back, but he could not then see the man at all.

His brother and the other man went down to the strand but could find neither the body nor the spectre. They made as much headway as they could with loading up, and soon their haul was up on the cart and away with each of the three of them as fast as the jennet could be persuaded to move.

They told everyone they met what Jack had seen and enquired if anyone else had seen the apparition, for nobody doubted the veracity of Jack's story, nor the terror that had been struck into him at the water's edge by what he had seen.

The old people they asked, who had seen more than the three men combined in their years on Earth, said Jack should have lifted the body away from the water and that is why the dead man followed him. He was seeking safety after his time in the water.

Searchers found the body eventually and buried it in a plot reserved for victims of the sea in the parish graveyard, but it was a long time before Jack Whitty or his kin could be persuaded alone onto that strand, or any other, either. Gathering material from the sea for a living is one thing, but dealing with ghosts of drowned sailors who follow you in broad daylight is quite another.

Being scared in daylight is a mighty thing, but the same sounds and tricks of the light that torment you in daylight can assume horrific proportions once darkness has spread over the countryside, as can be seen in the following tale gathered by Patrick Fleming in Ferrybank National School in the 1930s and recorded in the Irish Folklore Commission Collection.

During the time of the body snatchers in the early nineteenth century, Midi Twomey was employed to guard Slieverue graveyard every night. Micil, as he was properly known, often boasted that, though he was a small man, he did not fear ghosts. Boasting is easy until you are challenged.

The 1752 Murder Act said only corpses of executed murderers could be used for dissection by doctors and medical men when studying the human form. And since there was a limited supply of such bodies, body snatchers stole the fresh corpses of newly deceased persons for sale and no questions were asked. While the robbers and their clients dealt in bodies, they were not involved in taking lives, so the offence was treated as a misdemeanour if they were hauled before the courts.

The notorious exceptions were William Burke and William Hare, who in 1820s Edinburgh killed seventeen people so they could sell their bodies. Both were Irish migrant workers: Burke was from Strabane and Hare from Poyntzpass. Hare turned evidence against Burke in return for immunity against prosecution. Burke was subsequently hanged in 1829 and his body given over for dissection afterwards.

For all who died, by whatever means, midnight seems to be the witching hour when the restless dead may stir about. It happened to Midi that one night at about that time he heard a rattle of chains. All the courage that he had publicly proclaimed left him, as well it might, and he was on his own with the dead in the graveyard. He ran and ran until he reached a streetlamp at the bend of the public road.

The noise followed him no matter how fast he went. His terror grew stronger. So great was his trepidation at the approaching horror and the chinking noises that he had to stop and lean against a lamp post for support. The light above threw a circle of light onto the ground and inside that he felt safe; but the darkness all around was greater than the brightness in which he was stranded.

If a watched pot boils slowly then the sound of chains from the darkness of a graveyard takes eternity to quieten. Not all that moves in a graveyard is on two legs, however, for presently a four-legged creature showed itself in the light of the street

lamp. It paused and looked at Midi who was now standing behind the lamp post.

Man and beast looked at one another for some time. Midi listened for the sound of the chains but silence reigned now here and in the graveyard a little distance away. He looked at the four-legged jennett that had come into the light to study him. The jennet seemed as surprised as the man at the sudden encounter at midnight on a country road. Midi recognised the animal as one that was owned by Mrs Kelly, a neighbour of his, down the road. It must have wandered off her smallholding, he thought, and here it was on the road to who knows where at the witching hour.

At least the awful rattling of chains has stopped, he thought to himself. And the drenching perspiration was beginning to dry on his back. Suddenly, a sharp breeze blew along the road and made him to shiver without quite meaning to do so, as if someone had walked on his grave. Then his heart skipped another beat; the chain had begun rattling again. The jennet moved and stopped and looked backwards in the direction that Midi was staring; but neither could see anything beyond the pool of light on the grey tarmac of road.

The animal moved again and the chain noise returned. It stopped when the jennet stopped. Midi looked down and suddenly realised that the beast must have crossed someone's grave as it had caught its hoof in a boundary chain. The grave stayed where it was but the chain had gone with the jennet. It was the chain clanking on the animal's hoof that had sent Midi racing down the road away from a ghost that was not there.

He stepped out from his hiding place and removed the chain from the animal. He slapped it on the rump, not harshly, to make it start heading home to Mrs Kelly's place. Midi walked slowly and cautiously back to the graveyard with the chain. Grave robbers he could deal with, loose animals were not too troublesome; but a loose chain would need to be replaced by morning before anyone saw that something had been removed from Slieverue graveyard while Midi Twomey was on watch.

He declined to look over his shoulder as he walked back into the graveyard. He did not want to have his fortitude challenged again, whether by a daft jennet on four legs or by something else on two.

Eighteen

FINDING PEOPLE
IN A FIELD

Strange things can happen at night, especially in the country where there is little or no illumination beyond the light from the stars or the moon, or what is reflected by your own eyes from whatever bit of light there is to be found in a landscape.

The rural electrification scheme of the twentieth century helped many people to find their way home when street illumination became widespread. Before that, people used to report they had been led astray in the darkness on their way to somewhere else. Whether they were or whether it was just a handy excuse for being out without legitimate reason, is hard to say.

Nicholas Fitzgerald, a seventy-four-year-old farm worker from near Foulksmills, in 1937 told folklorist Tom Carey that he had experienced the phenomenon himself. He said he had often heard tell of people going astray in the night, and that he knew several men that went astray in the Foulksmills area.

A man he knew was lost in a field. His name was Lar. Worse was to come for even though he knew every blade of grass in the field; he could not find the well-worn path going through the field. He spent the whole night going around the field, and in the end he didn't know where he was, at all. It was a night that might have frighted the bravest of men. The place was filled with leaping shadows – now big, now small; but none had any real form.

So, he sat down and waited till daylight came into the world. When morning arrived he was astonished to find himself sitting on Cloney's Bridge in Old Ross, about 3 or 4 miles away from where he had started.

It might seem fanciful, but Nicholas Furlong, his neighbour, said it was a true fact; he knew the man well, and had heard him tell the story twenty times. He could never make out how it happened. But that was where he was in the morning, nearly 4 miles away from where he should have been.

Mr Furlong added he went astray himself one night too, in much the same way. He was away seeing an uncle of his who lived about 3 or 4 miles from his place. He left to return home about nine o'clock, and arrived safely by half past nine, or thereabouts. However, he had to go out in the field to see some horses that he had out there.

He recalled it was a dry night, but fairly dark with neither moon nor anything else to light his way. Nonetheless, it was a grand night for rambling. Like his neighbour before him, Nicholas Furlong said he too thought there were thousands of people in the field with him. He told Tom Carey that he himself could hear the rumbling of voices all around him, and could feel people walking every way, but try as he might he could not see anyone.

Like his neighbour before him, he said he went all around the field to find the gate and could not do so. He supposed he went around the field a hundred times, in vain. He saw the ditch right enough but knew that was not the way to go. In the end, he sat down and took off his boots and socks; and in one minute could see the gate right in front of him and had no trouble at all finding the way. Only for that he supposed he'd have been in the field all night, and who knew where he would have been when it got light, miles away most likely, if he had gone over the ditch.

Some people swear that if you take your boots or your coat off that you will find the way, after a while, when you are confused and lost. Certainly, if you are caught up in a *ceo draoíchta*, a magical mist, turning your coat inside out and wearing it thus will help you out of the mist, even though you may find yourself many miles away, as Nicholas' neighbour did.

At least the crowds in the field were harmless enough, even if they were noisy. In the early parts of the twentieth century in the Milltown Grange area a man went to take a cow to a bull illegally in the night and saw something more menacing. In fact, so threatening and frightening was what he saw, that his companion took fright and ran away leaving the man with an unrequited cow on his hands, and a fearful spectacle before him. An eighty-seven-year-old Elizabeth Byrne told folklorist Jim Delaney in 1955 that she heard the story from older people forty years before the collector spoke to her.

Elizabeth Byrne told Relavey that, the father of a family came home one evening after a hard day's stacking. He was tired and wanted to rest, but his wife insisted he bring the cow to the bull in the 20 acres Moate's Meadows field in Orpen's Demesne at Monksgrange. Mr Butler, the Protestant minister, lived in Orpen's and he owned the bull. There was a cover charge for the services of the bull, which was paid to the minister. But they wanted to use the bull without permission, or payment.

Recognising there would be a terrible row if he was discovered, the man brought a workman by the name of Kavanagh with him. The pair travelled along as quietly as it is possible to do with a cow until they got to the field at Moate's Meadows, where the bull was in residence. They let the cow into the field and hoped consummation would be completed as soon as possible with positive results.

However, much like Lar and Nicholas, they too realised that there were people in the field, beside themselves. In this case, the bull's field was full of soldiers marching up and down with swords at their sides.

Whatever about the cowman's need to protect his charge and bring her safely home; Kavanagh the workman did not feel any obligation to stand there until the marching soldiers and their weapons arrived where he was standing. Kavanagh fled, as any intelligent person might reasonably be expected to do when faced with a numerous body of armed men and with nothing to face them with beyond a single wondering cow.

The cow's owner, unable to manage a bull and a cow and keep watch for a roused owner with the field full of armed marching spectres, had to withdraw from the encounter and bring the unfulfilled cow back home again.

There was a boreen beside the field and this he used as a sure way home. As he led the cow along he saw a frightened face peering out from a bush at him. It was Kavanagh, who had taken cover in the bush after deciding he would be unable to outrun the soldiers if they gave chase with drawn swords. The cowman stopped and said to Kavanagh that for two pins, he'd knock the head off him for running away. The sight of a headless helper running back through the field might have frightened even the marching soldiers.

A story is told of a headless man being seen elsewhere in the county by people out rambling at night, so it would not have been the first sighting of such of a thing. A headless man is said to walk from Burkes Hill to Burkstown Cross and they say the ghost is that of Jim Roche. In the Black and Tan's era of the early 1920s, during the war of independence, Jim Roche was coming home from town on a horse, so the story goes.

A group of Black and Tans hid in a ditch as they heard his horse's approach. They rushed out in front of the horse to stop the rider and to question him as to his reasons for being abroad at night. Although established to target the Irish Republican Army, which was fighting for independence, the Black and Tans were notorious for their numerous attacks on the civilian population.

The horse was startled by the sudden appearance of the armed men and it took fright, throwing its rider. Jim Roche fell on his head, and the unfortunate man's head is said to have then disappeared through the ground, torn from his body by the encounter with the unyielding soil. His headless body lay there, before the stunned paramilitaries. The horse bolted, galloped away and was never seen again.

The body of Jim Roche was taken up, without his head, and buried in Kelly's Rath. It is said that his head was never recovered from the depths of the earth where the night's escapade had driven it. It had buried itself.

Since then, his ghost has often been seen at night, sometimes walking the roads, sometime on the ditch behind which the Black and Tans had hidden, and at other times sitting on the bridge at Boland's. Sometimes, he was dragging a bough of a tree along with him, for some reason. Other times, his headless spectre was seen riding a horse before he disappeared through the ditch on the way to who knows where else?

Local man Ned Furlong tried to overtake him once; but the figure vanished into the ground, according to Ned. Joe Whelan reported seeing the headless man one night when he was going to visit his own father some distance away, but he did not succeed in making contact with the ghost of Jim Roche.

Whether it is invisible talking ghosts, lost trails, marching soldiers or men who have mislaid their heads, strange things can happen at night in the Wexford countryside where there is little or no illumination, and where imagination is often the only guide.

Nineteen

TRAMPING TO A WAKE

Most old houses long ago were thatched in a neat manner, for if they weren't they did not survive for long in a storm. The thatch was got from straw or reeds or rushes that grew along the local river's edge, and the ridge along the top of a thatched roof was plastered with lime mortar, both as for ornamental reasons and for practical use as an anchor. The height of a roof ridge in one house had a bearing on a wake where a travelling man travelled out of this world while enjoying the hospitality of one family.

Johnny Doran was an old travelling man whose best days were all behind him when he arrived at Bill Redmond's house. Travelling folk such as Johnny became scarce on the ground once the County Home Care System was introduced and old-age pensions and widows' pensions came into operation to give the elderly some financial independence. Before that, the poorer people looked for shelter in the farmer's barn or any suitable place that would keep them dry and warm for the night. Of a long winter's evening, neighbours congregated to the houses where such lodgings were given and they listened to the stories and anecdotes travelling people carried with them.

When morning came, the storyteller generally asked for some tea, milk or eggs to take with them on their journey to the next abode where they would seek lodging for a night or so, once more. However, while neighbours enjoyed the company and the entertainment, many women of the house dreaded their coming for it was almost impossible to get them away without giving them too much, for they took kind to their feeding and were never shy when it came to asking for something, or, complaining if matters were not to their satisfaction. If a good supply of drink was brought in by the neighbours they would sing and sometimes shout, and other times could become very rough in talk and manner, once the drink was on them.

However, Johnny Doran would not tell too many more stories or travel many more miles, people could see that on him. His long tweed coat scraped the ground when he walked. It had seen better days before it was given to him by a wellwisher. The hat Johnny wore was a soft one that was moulded to his skull, a skull that had not a blade of hair to cross it, for he was entirely bald. His boots were lined with so many old pieces of paper to cover the holes that it could be said he was walking on paper and not leather at all. He had a wheeze on his chest that he could make reverberate at any sound he needed for a story; but for all that, his lungs were not taking in as much oxygen from the surrounding air as his body required or needed for survival.

One night, he fell to eating a sup supplied by the woman of the house and the food brought back his courage somewhat, enough to allow him to sit in the chimney corner and to tell a story.

Johnny said he met a man one night who was at a wake at a house in the Boker in Wexford town, who witnessed what happened. An old traveller came into the wake at about one o'clock in the morning. He was tired and hungry. While hospitality was supplied at wakes to all callers, some people frowned on feeding someone who did not know the corpse at all, and who had never exchanged a word of conversation with the dead person while they were alive.

When the old traveller came into the kitchen the place was crowded. The turf fire was ablaze and the flames were shining on the well-swept hearth and floor, and on the clean pewter and delft plates on the dresser. The kitchen table was taken up with people sitting all around it and talking rings around them. Nobody paid any heed to the man until someone took pity on him and took down a big lump of meat out of the cupboard, put it between two rough cuts of bread and gave it to the man.

Drink was taken and some of the fellows sitting around the table began teasing the traveller. However, others condemned their actions and said that they should show more respect. A row started and seasoned wounds were opened once more. The row became a boxing match that spilled out into the yard. Sometimes rows like that would start at a wake, but the pugilists always kept it quiet for fear of disrespecting the dead.

In a separate part of the house, the old man was asked for a loan of his scarf for the corpse. While we all like to believe that we will draw our last breath in a peaceful manner, with our chaste arms folded across our chest, like a pharaoh of old, the fact is that life departs the body at strange times, not caring what happens to its old corpse on its journey to somewhere else.

This corpse had died sitting up staring at the bedroomed door with arms outstretched and a look of panic on the slack-jawed face. And since there was nobody in the room at the time or for a while afterwards, his bones had fairly set in the shape they found him. They were able to lie him down on his back but his knees were in the air at that. So they borrowed the scarf and tied it around his bent legs to hold them down underneath the white sheet over him.

Once the old man was fed and had a small drop of clear liquid in his belly and in his head, he said it was time for him to be going. Most people were outside by then silently watching the fools' fight or trying to stop it before the family discovered what was going on, so few paid any attention to him.

He stepped into the empty wake room and, spying his scarf sticking out from a corner of the bed, he tugged at it. A scarf for a man of the road is not an adornment; it is an essential item of clothing used to keep warm and to keep a cold wind away from his chest. It served duty as well for many other uses when a ligature might be called for, or a bundle of sticks was needed for a fire.

Whoever had tied the scarf had tied it with a slip knot that unravelled as soon as the loose end was pulled. The legs of the corpse, no longer restrained, assumed what was for them now a natural formation. This in turn caused the corpse to sit up again, which meant the tie under his jaw slipped down.

When the old man, who was by now experiencing a certain swaying from the perpendicular himself, saw this development he wrapped the scarf around his own neck, tidied the ends in under his armpits and tightened his belt and departed the scene.

On his way out he passed the widow, a fine big woman, heading for the wake room. She of course screamed at the unexpected resurrection of her husband and that brought more people to the scene, who were also shocked to see the corpse rise from the bed. Most ran out into the night with such velocity that the fighting fools were submerged in a sea of humanity. Others ran in and asked what had happened, for it was plain to them that the dead man was still dead even if he had moved around the bed a little of his own accord.

The old man of the road took to his legs like a youngster and was well into the next parish by the time the candles were picked up from the floor and re-lit around the corpse – who had been wrestled back down to his proper repose by friends of the fighting fools, who by then were beginning to think of the road home and the safety of their own beds.

Many that left that night stopped off in the kitchen to pour a little salt into their pocket to throw at anything they met in the dark, in case they would be led astray on the way home.

There Johnny Doran's story ended, to general good humour in Bill Redmond's house. But, strange to relate, more than one of the departing neighbours took a pinch of salt with them on the way out Redmond's door, before stopping to take a drop of holy water from the font on the door frame to bless themselves with the water as they stepped out into the dark night.

The Redmond's house had a bed in the kitchen that was placed by the fire. It could be closed up like a box or a table in daytime. People called such beds a settle-bed or a box-bed. It was opened and folded out for Johnny on this night. The house fell silent and all slept through the night.

For Johnny it was his final sleep, for when Máire Redmond shook him the following morning for breakfast he was already well on his way on the long journey of the soul. His body was as stiff as the man's in his story had been.

This presented a dilemma for the couple, for if Johnny died in their home he was entitled to be waked there, but it was a working house and they needed to prepare for market. The income from the next market would meet the rent due on the holding. Bill solved the problem by bringing in an old door from the shed that, like Johnny, had seen better days. He tied a rope to each of the four corners and tied a fifth and longer piece of rope to the high roof of the house.

Johnny was placed, with due respect, on the door and after a moment of prayer and reflection the door and Johnny were hoisted up into the roof. The hoisting rope was tied off and there Johnny stayed for the day. If he was not quite in heaven he was on his way there.

That evening when the neighbours returned to mourn the passing of the storyteller, the door was lowered and Johnny was placed on the bed to be waked until daylight lit up the small window, once more. When all had departed, the door was hoisted once more and there Johnny Doran stayed until he was lowered, finally, for his second night of traditional waking in an Irish cottage.

He was buried the next day in a special corner of the parish cemetery, which was reserved for wandering people like him who had nobody to claim his body.

All he left behind him were his stories, which Johnny would have said was enough.

Twenty

HALLOWE'EN TRICKERY

The eve of All Hallows' Day is as important as the following day may be to wandering souls. The traditional celebration focuses on 31 October, beginning at sundown. A great many customs have grown up around the evening, which is known as Hallowe'en in some parts, and tales of strange goings on on this night are plentiful.

Elizabeth Byrne, an eighty-seven-year-old housewife in Rathnure, told folklorist Jim Delaney of Phil Connors, a queer old fella who lived long before the narrator told her story in the first place. His house was a place where people gathered to play card games and to chat. Phil was mostly alright and a decent enough host; but one Hallowe'en he abruptly said they would play no more cards that night because the holy souls would be around the house to visit at midnight. Before they knew where they were, he had put the bemused card players out of the house, saying that it would be an awful thing if the souls of all the people that ever lived in the house were now sitting on the shelves on the wall or on the dresser or the bars of the fire, and anywhere they could find a seat, and looking on at what the card players were doing.

Once they were gone and the voices had faded away, Phil gathered up all the well-handled cards and counted up that there were fifty-two cards plus jokers there; satisfied, he put them in a tobacco tin and put that inside the drawer of the blue-painted oak dresser nearest to the fireplace, whose firelight reflected dancing patterns on the willow-pattern dishes and coloured mugs, and on two china cups, a wedding present of long ago.

Phil, in putting the cards away, remembered only too well the game that had been played with two suits of diamonds and clubs when a joker had removed all the hearts and spades from the box and replaced them with identical suits. The row went on for days afterwards, causing Phil to bar everyone from the Connors' household while new cards were ordered in the local shop, upon which they were securely collected from the shopkeeper by Phil himself.

Phil set a basket of potatoes on the open fire to boil. While waiting for them to cook, he swept the hearth well so that there was no dust nor bits of turf, nor coal, nor half-burnt twigs left anywhere that they should not be by the time he was finished. He left the kitchen ready for the poor souls, whom he was convinced would be calling to their home, come the turning of the day at midnight.

He and his wife went to bed. We do not know her name; but it would be safe to assume she was known to at least some of the locals as Mrs Phil.

It wasn't long before sleep overcame them, perhaps out of ecstatic expectation or apprehension, who can tell at this remove. When all was quiet and both were snoring away like corncrakes in a meadow, the card players, who had not gone further than the far wall of the yard, returned to the lime-washed cottage, lifted the latch and stepped in. They found the potatoes and ate as many as they could without choking while laughing. Bellies full beyond bearance, they took the rest away with them.

Hard times breed hard men, and hard men make rough manners. There wasn't a skin or a morsel left behind when they stepped out into the night to join the milling souls, ghosts, good people and all who were abroad on Hallowe'en in County Wexford and beyond.

The following morning dawned quietly enough with just the sound of the hens to be heard, pecking around outside the door in the hope of finding something being thrown out for them to eat by Mrs Phil.

An awakened Phil rolled out of the narrow double bed first to see if the candles could be extinguished now the night had passed in safety. He wandered sleepily enough into the kitchen; but he was soon wide awake and come to his senses at what he saw in the kitchen. He saw nothing at all, which was what perplexed him entirely.

When two people are married for a long time they often don't need to talk or to call out to one another to be heard. For Mrs Phil it was enough that her man was not grumbling and kicking the hind leg of the sugán chair nearest the door, which they had inherited from her bachelor uncle. The uncle never thought much of Phil, while he was alive, and it was Phil's indulgent habit to kick the leg of the chair in lieu of kicking the dead man when he was down.

A perturbed Mrs Phil tumbled out of bed in the silence and stood at the door to the kitchen, looking not unlike one of the living dead that were reputed to be abroad on the night before this. Her torso, legs and hair had seen softer times. In this she matched her husband who was by now well hacked about by life.

Phil cried his thanks to God, and told his wife that the Holy Souls were there on the night before, for they did not leave a potato in the place. He truly believed this and that night, added a decade of the rosary to the nightly recital for five of the most neglected souls in Purgatory who had nobody to pray for them. Mrs Phil joined in, though she suspected it was mortal mouths that had eaten her week's supply of spuds, especially when the card players returned with smiles as wide as men who had not put off thatching until the storm was at hand.

They were well fed and had one up on Phil Connors whom they prevailed upon, *ad nauseum*, to re-tell the story of the eaten potatoes of Hallowe'en. Which he did, every time on request, knowing in his own being that the wandering souls had chosen his home on that one night to come and take sustenance.

Nothing ever shook his belief that he had been chosen. He told people this, and terrified more than a few as he reached the end of his own life by saying that he would come back at Hallowe'en to his own place to partake of a plateful of potatoes, once matters were settled in the other place.

That was Phil Connors' story.

People in other parts of the county had different ways of celebrating Hallowe'en, according to Patrick Kennedy in his work *Evenings in the Duffrey* on Wexford ways. He recalled that in one townland, when supper was over most of the people that were assembled in the house went out into the yard to begin the ceremonies of the night. They broke a cake into several parts, and everyone took a portion of cake in hand and lined up before the door. The first flung his piece against the door and cried out for hunger to go away to the Sassenach till this night twelvemonth; the next person did the same, and so on to the last, until all done. They then went in, and sat round the big hearth on stools and bosses, chattering away and laughing.

The women of the house brought out bags of apples and others of nuts that they had held over from the harvest, and laid them on the table. They bade the assembly to enjoy themselves until they were tired.

The nuts and apples were shared among the company and games were played. More importantly, an iron stand was set up over the fire and the gathering began to try the fortunes of different couples who were spoken of as sweethearts, to see what the next year might bring to them. Different pairs of nuts were set side-by-side on the iron stand sitting atop the fire, one representing a young man and the other his sweetheart. As the heat rose in the nuts they would burst open. If the nut representing the girl burst open first and flew off, his chance was over; he was finished. Likewise, if his nut were to burst first, it was the same with her, he was lost to her. However, if both nuts burned side by side and popped at the same time, they would be married. Of such veracities were marriages made one time in parts of County Wexford.

Twenty-one

DANCING IN
DARKNESS

Why is it that the Devil always seems to appear at dances? Is it because humans dance close to one another when the lights are low and, with a bit of encouragement from a loitering imp, could be persuaded to indulge in a little sin? Or is it a pishogue put about by people whose dancing days are over, and who would prefer if nobody was out dancing now that they are not dancing themselves? An easy way to frighten anyone is to say 'the Devil is afoot; mind yourself and come home early'.

Long ago, people walked to dances and everyone knew everyone else as a consequence, so if there was anything amiss all would know about it soon enough. Then the bicycle was invented and the world changed forever. Where people were once limited by the distance they could walk of an evening, dance for hours on end, and walk home again; now people could cycle for miles out of their own areas to attend a dance with strangers – where the opportunity for anonymous high jinks was boundless. Shy-enough girls could makes eyes at likely lads and lads could strut their stuff without fear of ridicule from neighbours in their own place. Nonsensical wrestling matches between young stags could be resolved by one of them vaulting onto a bike and cycling away into the night, making both protagonists a winner and no harm done.

Girls cycled together and fellas cycled in gangs in great clouds of perspiration to the dances. Is was easy to find where a dance might be held at any time for there would be bicycles. Bikes going there, bikes stopped on the side of the road with a chain gone astray, bikes freewheeling while their owners chatted to others intent on the same course of action. Not to mention bikes thrown up on a grassy bank abandoned for the time being while their riders were otherwise engaged.

The cycling and the dancing worked up a fierce hunger, so tea and ham suppers were provided (at an extra cost) by the dance organisers for partaking of during the interval, or whenever it suited a fella to ask a girl if she would like something to eat. If she said yes, they were on their way to somewhere. But not every young man or young woman who went to dances wanted to become serious enough to share a ham tea with someone; most made do with a warm bottle of minerals drunk through a straw and the sharing of a small packet of sugared biscuits with pals.

Dances were held outdoors when weather permitted and indoors when there was no alternative. In time, concrete-block dancehalls were built, but for years before that any venue with a flat floor would serve. There were few enough places with a sprung floor to dance on, so if bodies were aching for days afterwards it was not always from the exertion of cycling. When pounding feet hammered the earth it was not always the earth that gave way.

In one parish the dance was held on a farm, in a barn where the geese used to have squatters' rights. On dance nights they were evicted from their nesting place and humans poured in to take their places. No geese were allowed back into the barn and they instead wandered out and around the haggard and made a desperate noise. Since geese do not dance with one another for recreation, they were at a loss as to why they were evicted from their usual haunt.

Alice Flaherty wanted to go to her first dance at seventeen years of age and was very excited because she had recently earned some cash teaching Irish to a Protestant boy whose school did not teach the language. The cash was now ear-marked for her first dance.

She was invited to go to the dance by a schoolteacher's wife who liked to dance but whose husband was not a great dancer and would not go. The woman wrote a letter and gave it to Alice to show to her mother to see how matters might fare.

The mother took the letter into another room so she could study each word and be sure the letter was indeed written by a schoolteacher's wife. Alice would be seventeen years old on Saturday and the dance would be held on Sunday. It would make a wonderful birthday present for her eldest daughter – but Alice's mother wanted to be sure there would be no mishap to create a bad impression on her daughter's big night out. She could find no fault with the letter and knew the teacher's wife, Elinore, to be an upstanding member of the community, so she gave her permission to Alice.

Sunday came and Alice went down to Elinore's house in the afternoon to prepare for the dance. The hall they were using was in the other parish and was a half hour's cycle away, so they set out at about seven o'clock so as to be there when the music started at eight. It was a fine summer's evening and the road was freckled with sunlight and shade where the sun shone

through the leaves of the trees overhead. Alice was excited
and full of questions as they cycled along. When was Elinore's
first dance? When did she learn to dance? Did she know every
dance there was to know? What was Vienna like, with all the
waltzes? How could they dance with such full dresses without
tripping and falling over?

Elinore laughed at the questions as they topped a hill that
Alice had not even noticed in her excitement. She said she
was never in Vienna, only barely knew how to dance a proper
waltz and, if she was to take the time to learn all the dances
that could be learned, then she would be so old that nobody
would want to dance with her.

Alice chatted on, her tongue keeping time with her flash-
ing legs. That is, until she fell silent and began to look at the
ground; Elinore knew they must have arrived and that there
were boys studying all approaching females from the safety of
the wall opposite the hall. Elinore was not long about shush-
ing them away and she and Alice entered the hall of dreams.

The night began, the music spilled into their heads and male
after male asked Alice to dance, until her head was in such a
spin she knew not whether it was time to dance or time to sit
down. On Elinore's advice she declined offers of ham teas and
packets of biscuits and bottles of minerals from a great many
people. She had no recollection, for a week afterwards, as to
how she got home. She simply knew she was delivered safely to
her mother's door by a laughing Elinore.

Once started, Alice and Elinore became a dancing part-
nership; that is to say, they travelled to dances together and
Elinore kept an eye on her young charge as men, young and
old alike, flocked about her. One young, dark-haired man
whose English name was Frederick but whose Irish name was
Fear Dorcha, the Dark Man, paid Alice particular attention.
However, for all his blandishments, Alice was not nearly

ready for a singular relationship with one man over all the suitors she had flocking about her, no matter how good looking or personable he was.

Alice did not see Frederick after the night she told him she was too busy for a ham tea and wanted to keep dancing. However, a mysterious event happened at the Camolin bonfire night and Alice wondered if the man involved had been her Frederick. It was said that a boy and a girl who had been dancing together all evening and into the early hours of the morning left the ground in a blaze of flame while the other dancers stood and watched in amazement. Try as people

might, they could not find the girl again. She belonged to a family in Kilkenny and had only arrived in the area that day, and had no kin to speak up for her. Some said the dark-haired boy was the Devil, but who knows?

A more believable story came from Nash bonfire night when a spirited girl wanted to keep dancing for as long as she could stand up, but found the other dancers were wandering away as the bonfire faded away into ashes. She implored them to stay, saying that she would find more wood to keep the fire burning. She went to a graveyard in search of firewood. The only burnable wood to be had in the cemetery were some old crosses that lay on their sides, marking the old graves where few mourners came to tend to their dead.

The girl, supposing they would not be missed, gathered some broken crosses and, returning to the bonfire, flung them onto the embers. A scream ripped through the air and the girl was seen to rise up and disappear into the clouds. She was not seen again.

These stories soon enough spilled over from the dancers to the people in the homes in the towns and villages, and out in the country. Dances were ended earlier as if that would fool the Devil into thinking it was not worth his while to go to the dances in search of souls.

Alice's mother heard the stories, as did Elinore's husband, the schoolteacher. He spoke to Elinore and they decided that, for now, it was not a good idea for the schoolmaster's wife to be seen attending dances where there was a danger the Devil might turn up on a bicycle. Once Elinore no longer went, Alice could not go to the dances, and so her brief spell as the belle of the ball was over. But for ages afterwards her dreams were taken up by swirling dancers and the smile of a dark man who had asked her to sit with him and whom she had refused, for good or ill.

Twenty-two

FAUST AT
THE FORGE

There was once an old nun living in Maudlinstown who was so holy that the Devil himself came to tempt her into breaking her vows. She said that God had told her to fast for some number of days, to see if she would obey him. She took her vow of obedience seriously and so began to fast, according to Madge Browne, a pupil of The Faythe Convent School Wexford in 1938, who got the story from her friend Lily Meyler.

One day, the good nun was praying in her room when something scratched or scrawbed her skin, leaving scratches and droplets of blood on her white flesh. There was a faint throb of pain from the wound but not enough to seek medical assistance. She reported what had happened to her sisters in prayer, and said that she was sure she had not seen anything enter her fasting room where she was at prayer. They reflected on the account she had given but concluded that it must have been the house cat that had caused the damage.

She accepted their consensus and, when she returned to her room, made sure the door was locked securely against intrusion. But locked doors will not keep out demons, for it was the Devil that had entered the room in the first place; it was the Devil that had scrawbed her skin with sharp nails. She knelt to pray once more and tried to ignore the hunger pangs that echoed in the rumbling of her empty stomach.

When next the Devil appeared to her he did so as a man, dressed in beautiful garments. He said if she did not eat she would die soon. He said that God did not want her to be greater than himself and God wanted her to die to prove he was almighty. The starving nun remained unmoved by his argument and said she would keep her promise to God to fast.

But a human is mortal. The Devil continued to tempt the starving nun so much that she eventually gave in to his blandishments and cunning persuasions in her weakened state, and accepted the food he offered her. But if she thought she had the upper hand with the Devil in a house of religion and faith, she was sorely mistaken. She dropped down dead on the spot as soon as she tasted the food. The Devil, far from leaning down to see what had happened to her, laughed in triumph at her prostrate body, for now he had her soul for himself, forever and ever.

He tried his hand once more in another part of Wexford – where exactly we don't know – but we do know that the story was told by Henry Condon of Carrickbyrne to Josie Kehoe of Carrigbyrne School, in Newbawn in 1938, and it is in the Irish Folklore Commission Collection.

There was a blacksmith living in County Wexford at one time and he was very poor. His forge was near a crossroads. It was a small forge with a slated roof over it and a door divided into two parts to allow heat to escape over the half door in summer, and to keep out the cold wind that came in winter to deaden the ankles. There was one big fireplace in the forge and a pair of bellows made of timber and leather, which were kept beside the fireplace. There was also a poker, used by the smith for stirring the fire, tongs to take the red iron out of the fire and a hammer to make the iron into the shape of the horseshoe. The smith shoed horses and asses, though not cattle. This was the way of life that had proceeded for generations.

One day, a gentleman came riding on a horse right up to the forge door. The smith heard him coming and knew the horse to be a well-born animal by the sound of his strut and clop. The blacksmith stepped outside the forge, he rubbed his oversized hands on his leather apron and waited for the other to speak. The rider looked down at him with the eye of one who had been a long time travelling to this place. He spoke in a deep voice that everyone in the forge had little trouble hearing. He asked the blacksmith to shoe his horse. He dismounted and unsaddled the horse before the smith led it inside to work on the new shoe.

Work completed, the perspiring smith asked the well-dressed gentleman for his payment. He waited and watched, for he knew this was no ordinary man nor any horse he had ever tapped a shoe nail into in his mortal life. The black-clad rider gave the smith £100 in coins in a purse. It was a fortune at the time and more than the smith would receive for shoeing the horse of any lord for miles around. More, even, than he would accumulate in a lifetime of heat and grinding sweat.

The blacksmith counted the money away from the curious eyes of the hangers-on at the forge: they who did not own a horse nor an ass among them but who warmed themselves at his fire all day and who took home glowing coals at evening as fire starters to their own cold houses. They whose curious eyes were bulging from their heads with want of knowing his business.

He spoke quietly to the man who had come to him this day with this black shining animal, and asked why he was being paid so much for his work? The stranger spoke so softly that but one person could hear what he had to say. He told the smith that the purse was his to keep – but the smith would have to come with him in ten years time when he returned for his soul. For it was Lucifer standing there in the warm yellow daylight.

He thought about it for a while and then said he would do so, when the time came; meanwhile, he would use the wealth in his hands to make his life more comfortable. This he did and he told nobody what had passed between him and the dark stranger, no matter what way they came at him with questions.

But before the ten years were up an angel came to the blacksmith. The angel came in the form of a lady on a pony and trap with a driver. She stepped down from the gentle green trap and spoke softly to the smith. She said to him that he had become very rich, more rich than a blacksmith might expect to be. There must have been somebody here who gave you money, she said without preamble, for she knew that he recognised who she was. The blacksmith told her the Devil had been there, to which the angel replied he should not have taken anything from the Devil. Reluctant to forgo his good fortune, the smith talked around the matter for a while. He explained he did not know it was the Devil at his forge until he had the horse shod for him, but he left out the bit about the use of his own free will as to whether to take the money or not in the first place. He made the point that he had agreed to go with his benefactor when the time came.

The angel said she would help and gave him a snuffbox. It was a small green box with a trim of gold leaf and a snug-fitting lid with a gold clasp on the front. She explained that whoever stepped into that box could not leave it until the blacksmith told him that he might. In case the enchanted box was not enough for him, the angel also told him that anyone who climbed up on the apple tree behind the forge could not leave until the smith would allow him to do so.

When the ten years were up, the Devil came along, though not in as much finery as on his first appearance. The blacksmith bade him to sit on his armchair for it was a special chair made long ago by an ancestor, before he was even born. Once a person sat in it, iron hoops came out around the waist and they were trapped until a lever behind the chair was released. Very often it was a way of getting non-payers to settle their smithy debts on the spot.

The Devil sat in the chair while the blacksmith dilly dallied as long as he could. By then, the Devil could not get out of the chair. He asked the smith to let him go, offering not to return for him for ten more years. The smith let him go.

Ten years were not long going once more. The Devil came along, this time with fifty young devils in tow, for surety. The old Devil declined to go in to take hold of the smith so the young devils went in. However, the blacksmith, being in no hurry to be off to Hell, kept the young devils waiting for such a long time that, at last, the old fella went in.

The cunning smith bet the Devil that, despite his great powers, he would not be able to get into the box the angel had given him. Of course, the Devil said he could and, what's more, he took the half a hundred young devils in with him for company. The triumphant smith closed the lid of the angel's box and would not let them out, no matter how much they banged around inside the box, until the thwarted Devil once more agreed that if the smith let him out he wouldn't come back for another ten years.

The third ten years were not long going and the Devil came along, this time determined that he would take back his prize soul. The smith could think of no way to avoid the bargain, so he agreed to go with the Devil, who was mightily pleased with himself, as you might well imagine.

The tired blacksmith had forgotten all about the apple tree and the angel. He locked the door of the forge, for he would not be back to shoe a horse there ever again, and stepped out to go off with the Devil. However, when they were passing by the bowed down apple tree the Devil, remembering the origin of sin in the Garden of Eden, went up the tree for the juiciest of apples at the top, just to show that he was master of all. Of course, he could not then get down again.

The Devil was in the apple tree for two long months until the blacksmith at last relented and let him down again.

A relieved Devil left the forge and never came back. The angel's box vanished and, when the smith glanced in the Devil's purse, he found that the remaining money had turned into autumn leaves that crumbled when he touched them. Still, better the loss of the Devil's coins than the loss of his immortal soul.

The smith lived on at the forge for many years to follow and in his turn grew old and slower. He yielded place in the forge to his son – but warned him to be on the lookout for a dark stranger on a sleek black horse.

Twenty-three

HURLING DAYS AT LOUGH CULLEN

Hurling is on a par with breathing for Wexford people. Every Wexford child knows that hurling is a unique Irish game and one of the oldest and fastest field games in the world.

Cúchulainn, the warrior hero of Irish mythology, was given his name when he killed a fierce guard dog, which was attacking him at the time, by driving a sliothar down its throat with a well-struck shot from his hurley. He was berated by the villagers for killing the hound, which had belonged to Culann the blacksmith and so Setanta, as he was known at the time, undertook to find another animal and train it for Culann. In the meantime, he acted as Culann's guard and so became known to all as Cúchulainn, the Hound of Cullen.

Not every hurler has been called upon to kill a dog with a hurling ball, but some have tried to take the life of an opponent in the heat of battle. By the Middle Ages, hurling was being played between different parishes with teams of up to thirty players taking part. It wasn't until the Gaelic Athletic Association (GAA) was formed in 1884 – and put manners and rules on the confrontation – that counties had the chance to play each other under set rules. Even then, with a rulebook in place, there were still rows and ructions over transgressions.

Some years before the meeting in Thurles that set up the GAA, a cross-country football match was played at a point between Kilmacow and Vanrog, which would have been similar to hurley in the application and enthusiasm of the players – not that Wexford men needed outside encouragement to get stuck in.

The number of men on each side was thirty, more or less, according to Patrick Byrne of Ballincrea, Slieverue, whose version of what occurred is recorded in the Irish Folklore Commission Collection. The experience of the match was more akin to a war of invasion, conquest and resistance than the conventional scoring of goals and points with a referee on hand to adjudicate. Each team from the opposing parishes strove to end the game by gaining possession of the other's heartland; that is to say, where they lived during the week.

The elder folk of both Kilmacow and Vanrog, whose galloping days were at an end, gave opinion and advice to the players on their own teams, sometimes followed, sometimes ignored; the attention or non-attention to which only became an issue on the outcome of the game for victor or vanquished.

The game was played on Sunday, as was usual for leisure pursuits at the time, given that Saturday was a working day for most people. The match lasted for a long and furious two hours. Sunday dinner, then taken at noon, was swallowed in haste, after which the players hurried rather than ran with hurlies in hand to the field. There, in a state of intense perspiration, and after the terrible exercise of two hours battling implacable foes, they threw themselves motionless on the green grass to refresh, with heaving lungs, their life force, aching bones and tired-out muscles.

To begin the game, one team captain pitched up his hurley in the air and caught it neatly as it came down; he held it out at arm's length, grasping it at the precise spot that it met his palm in its descent. The other captain took hold of it, his hand resting on the other's; he, letting go his hold, fixed his grasp immediately above his opponent's hand. Finally, the thumb and first finger of one coming within one inch of the top, the other player seized the hurley by the small remaining portion and, swinging it three times round his head, was adjudged the first choice for best position.

The ball used was a long narrow ball. A tall fat man named Angus, who played with Kilmacow, won every match for them and did so once more on this occasion by going into Vanrog before the Vanrog men could swing the contest into Kilmacow. Vanrog had to be content to live to fight on another day.

Curiously, the same storyteller, Patrick Byrne, recorded a story about a lake by the name of Loch Cullen, a name not a million miles away from Cúchulainn. The site where the lake is today was at one time a flat plain, and was where massive games of hurling took place.

One day, two teams of hurlers were arranged in line and fronting each other about ten ridges apart, when an independent spectator, taking the heavy leather-covered ball of about 3lbs weight, flung it high between the lines, and at once dozens of hurlies were brandished. They rose into the air like pikes of war and a rush like a battle charge took place towards the supposed spot of its meeting the ground. Several aimless swings and muscle-bruising blows were made as it descended with increasing speed. One champion's hurley, wielded by his muscular arms, received it on the broad curved end with a heavy stunning sound as the hurley met the ball. The ball flew back into the clouds, to make its next descent at the distance of half the field away.

By and by, one of the hurlers grew thirsty from the exertions. He left the playing field and went searching for water. While he was searching he met a witch, though he did not know she was a witch. He asked where he would find water. She pointed to a holly bush and told him if he would lift the bush he would have water in plenty. But, she warned him, when he was finished drinking his fill he must be careful to replace the bush again. The man went and found the water beneath the bush just as she had said. He drank his cold fill until his sleek belly ballooned with water and his tongue shrank back to normal size – but he forgot to return the bush to where he had removed it from the earth. Unconcerned, he returned to his companions. It is said the water from the holly poured out and out without pause or pulse until it formed a lake of new water that nobody could prevail against. The man, the witch and the hurlers were all drowned, according to Patrick Byrne of Ballincrea.

John O'Donovan, the great Irish scholar of the nineteenth century, had a slightly different version. He said that, according to popular belief, Tory Hill, which rises over Loch Cuileann, was formerly a theatre of pagan worship for the people of the surrounding county. On one occasion, pagan worship being completed, athletic contests commenced. The people were assembled on the *faiche*, or plain, which extended up to the border of the thick wood. Women and girls occupied the portion next to the road, as the direction of the play was parallel to that side, and they would be out of harm's way. They were there to encourage and admire the flying limbs of the men whose days were otherwise passed in physical labour.

At that time, O'Donovan said, hurling teams were of the order of sixty players a side with hurleys made of holly and hazel. In a twist to the story, He said there was a wicket at both ends: goals through which a team scored.

The teams rushed at each other like the wind; one team tried to speed it to the goal near the fence of the field on that side, the other attempted to arrest its progress and send it back. One player would send it flying back over the heads of the mingled forces of both teams. That would send the confused tide backward as fleetly as it came forward. Seldom was an opportunity for an unencumbered stroke to be had by a player from either side, such was the galloping intention of all players.

One of the hurlers turned off the hurling green to quench his thirst, but, not finding any water, wandered about in search of a well or a spring that might offer some cooling water for him to drink. Tragically for all, he was met by a witch in disguise, who told him there was no well near at hand but that if he went over to the tuft of rushes which she pointed to and pulled one rush from there, a well of pure water would issue from the earth from which he might slake his thirst.

He did so, the rush coming away quite easily in his hand, but such a flood of water issued from the soft ground that it overflowed the plain and drowned, not only the thirsty youth, but all of his unsuspecting companions on the hurling green.

It is further narrated by O'Donovan that for succeeding ages afterwards, when the full moon arose over the calm surface of the placid lake, ghost players could be seen hurling on its surface. The exultant shouts of the victorious and the defiant cries of the vanquished could be heard echoing back and forth. The waters of the lake became unusually agitated while the match progressed, until the hurlers seemed to sink beneath the water once more, and the night air was still again, save for the voice of the enchantress exultingly calling: '*An luachair! An luachair!*', 'the rushes, the rushes'.

She alone had her way.

Twenty-four

ARRIVAL OF
THE ANTICHRIST

In a time when stories of giants roaming the land were common and priests and ministers of religion warned that the Day of Judgement was on its way a week next Friday, a woman witnessed the arrival of the Antichrist on the road outside of her house, near the village of Kilmore in County Wexford.

Theresa was going about her normal business of searching for a clucking hen in the long nettles at the back of the house, when she became aware of a presence above her and looked up. It was more of a shadow that had come across where she was beating nettles down with a long stick than a sound that attracted her attention.

What she saw there caused her to call her husband Tom, to witness the moment of realisation. Tom stepped into the bright light of day from the darkness of their house, and eye-lids blinked in involuntary protest, for he could not believe his eyes, either. No doubt about it, said Tom to himself, there was not one but six Antichrists on the road near the gate to the lower field staring back at him, saying not a word. Even his mongrel, Thunder, was too shocked to bark and was instead whining and crawling, belly to the ground.

Their house was not far from a model farm where fifteen people were employed and where a miller was kept just to run the farm's mill. The miller was a special person in farm hierarchy and while all others drank from tin mugs, the miller had a chaney mug to use at meal times to show he was special.

The owner of the farm, a Mr Parkes, took the business of running a model farm seriously and embraced improvements in agricultural techniques, efficiency and building layout. He was committed to the education of his workers and honoured a commitment to improving their welfare.

On Saturdays, when the week ended, the workmen were paid with two stone of barley meal each and a small amount of money as wages for their week's toil.

It was a busy place and a haunt for crows and other free-loaders who came to feed off the work in the growing fields. Crows were a particular problem. To deal with them, Parkes hired young lads to scare off the birds and to make sure they did not set up permanent colonies in the trees surrounding the land. Their task was to wait until birds gathered in sufficient numbers, and to then scare them away with as many stratagems as they could manage to press into practice.

One way to do so was to hang dead crows from trees and posts near the crops. A live crow would see only death, not food, and would stay away. Another way was to bang the lids on old pots given for that purpose by the cook. In other places they tied coloured ribbons to fence posts to fly and dance in the breeze, making the birds believe they were seeing flying snakes. For a while, they even placed a scarecrow in one field with a nailer's high hat on his head and outstretched arms inside an old dress. They moved it around each morning and the woollen dress flapped in the wind and kept the crows away. The dress and the wooden frame caused a great deal of merriment among the young men, which was to lead to what happened when the Antichrists appeared on the road later that day.

When the boys were not chasing away flapping crows they were employed to destroy thistles in the pastures. They carried salt to put on the heads of thistles, for salt acts as a desiccant, drawing moisture out of the plant and withering it to death. Since their work was mostly in the mornings and evenings, the crow-chasers found they had time on hand in the middle of a working day, which with young minds is a dangerous combination of circumstance.

It was a tradition at one time in Wexford that workers took a long break from their labours around noon and went to rest. Not only the men but women, children and servants ceased work and rested for about an hour or two, some stretching their time off to three o'clock of an afternoon, depending on their occupation.

On this day, Peadar, the leader of the crow chasers, went to see how the miller was getting on with his duties. He found the miller asleep and snoring among the empty sacks in the mill. He had been lulled to sleep by the warmth of the day and the pleasant sound produced by the revolving wheels and lapping water, as it passed from bucket to bucket in the wheel.

Peadar recalled a passing traveller telling a story of a miller's headstone he had seen in Nash graveyard in Cassagh, which said: 'Here lieth the body of Anthony Reynolds, a native of County Tyrone he was faithful to his employer and though a miller an honest man. Departed this life 13 December 1790 aged thirty-three years.'

Not to be outdone, Peadar, who had been schooled to reading and writing as far as second book, wrote on a piece of white cloth a similar epitaph for the miller before him and placed it on the man's rising and falling chest.

He wrote: 'Here lieth the body of Parkes' miller who though an honest man slept away his master's day.'

Departing the scene before the miller (a man well known for his quick temper) awoke, Peadar found his way to where his companions slept on bunches of dry grass at the foot of a very large and very old tree. Most of them were sleeping with their faces to the sod. Early mornings and late nights will take a toll on the human body, young or old, and most were glad to rest and fall into a light sleep until they were called to arms once more. Peadar amused himself for a while by untying their boot laces and retying them together, so the wearer would fall down when he tried to walk on awakening.

He was removed from his caprices by the farm's carpenter, who recognised in Peadar his own youthful giddiness and knew his victims would not thank Peadar for making them fall on their faces after a midday sleep. He called Peadar to his side and asked him if he would help complete a task, seeing that Peadar had decided not to rest on the grass with the others? Peadar, who wanted to be a craftsman on the farm, readily agreed and went with the carpenter to his workshop where the smell of freshly planed wood greeted his arrival.

The carpenter explained that he was to make half a dozen pairs of stilts for a play that was to be put on the following month, as part of a surprise birthday party for the farmer's wife. Six people were to come through the trees waving ribbons from the top of their tall hats as a surprise to the assembled guests. Did Peadar think he could assist the carpenter to put the finishing touches to the stilts?

Peadar said he was willing to help for as long as he could; but the carpenter would have to try and make do without him once the sleeping period was over for he had important duties to perform himself in keeping the crows away. The carpenter agreed to the terms and they were working happily away when there was a falling sound from the tree outside and shouts of confusion and anger came floating on the breeze to the carpenter's shop. Peadar feigned great interest in the grain of wood of one of the stilts and wondered if they would support the weight of a man, namely himself.

The vengeful noise of stomping feet was coming closer; the victims of the lace-tying experiment having concluded that if Peadar was the only one missing then he must be responsible for their misfortune. The search was on for him.

The carpenter hustled Peadar up on to a frame where hung a long pair of trousers. He rested the stilts below the trousers and bade Peadar slide his feet down inside the trousers. Uncertainly, Peadar stood up inside the trousers, which by then hid the stilts below from view.

Imagine the surprise of his companions when he emerged from the woodworking hut to stare down at them. They stopped, at a loss for words. They were envious of Peadar and his towering height; this was fun and they wanted to join in. Laces and bruised faces were forgotten, and it was not long before the carpenter had all six young lads kitted up on stilts with raggedy trousers hiding their wooden supports.

It was from this vantage point that Peadar saw the resurrected miller erupt from his mill in the distance, clenching a piece of cloth with some letters written thereon and looking for the culprit with murder in his eyes.

Quick as a flash, Peadar suggested to his companions that they try out their stilt legs in a direction diametrically opposite to the approaching miller. This led them to the gate of the homestead of Theresa and her good husband Tom. They had left the charging miller behind them and were intent on circling back to frighten the crows with this latest weapon of

theirs when they saw the woman and the man fall to their knees before them. Theresa pulled out her rosary beads and began to recite the rosary; Tom was not long behind her. She was not far into the saying of the rosary when she cried out to Tom that the Antichrists had arrived, six of them. She knew they would come, she said, for she had read it in the Prophecies.

Tom said nothing at all beyond wishing fervently that all of this would prove to be a dream and he would awake presently, a bit jaded perhaps, but otherwise fully *compos mentis*.

Both closed their eyes, the easier to pray with fervour and intensity. They went on so for a while in the silence of the day and, when they finished the prayers and opened their eyes, the six apparitions were gone.

In the distance they heard the sound of crows and in the sky they saw a great cloud of disturbed birds rising from the trees. They went inside, closed the door and poured out strong tea for themselves. Tom laced it with a sup of poitín for he knew not what else the day might bring. Very often, fortification is needed by ordinary people against whatever travels down the road to their house and home – especially when the Antichrist is about on the lanes of County Wexford and up to mischief.

Twenty-five

CROSSING
THE WATER

Stories have always been told of travellers finding their way blocked by a river or lake and having to obey the crossing protector or pay a ferryman for safe transport to the other side. The most famous perhaps is the Styx, a river in Greek mythology, which formed the boundary between Earth and the Underworld, or Hades. Charon, the ferryman, transported the souls of the newly dead across this river into the Underworld. Placing a coin in the mouth of the deceased paid the toll to cross the Styx, which led on to the entrance of the Underworld.

But that was a long time ago. A more recent ferryman was involved in a conversation with a number of legal bigwigs about crossing the Barrow to get to the other side. Among their number was the splendidly named Caesar Colclough.

In 1797, Colclough lived at Duffrey Hall, in the western section of the county, about 80 miles west of Enniscorthy. His family had extensive estates in the south of the county and were reputed to be among the more liberal Anglicans of the area, though he actively opposed the encouragement of insurrection in the county.

One day, a number of legal gentlemen of the Leinster circuit were waiting on the Kilkenny side of the ferry at Ballinlaw on the Barrow for a favourable moment to cross to the Wexford side. A storm was blowing and the river was angry. The ferryman was fearful for the safety of the crossing, but lucrative briefs lay on the other side of the river to be dealt with. The venture was worth the risk, agreed the legal eagles. Among the barristers was Colclough, who carried with him at all times on his journeys a pair of valued saddle bags. While the rest were hesitating, like timorous bathers with one toe in the water, Colclough impatiently flung his travelling bags onto the ferry and jumped aboard.

Charles Kendal Bushe, who later became a judge, recalled that while the shivering ragged boatman pointed out the danger inherent in casting off for the other side in such conditions, Colclough dismissed his fears with the cry: 'You carry Caesar and his saddle bags,' a reference to Julius Caesar and a similar reported occurrence from the days of the Roman Empire. Whether or not the boatman of the day was as familiar with Caesar and his Roman pronouncements as the story suggests, the saga was to take a more profound twist.

As they headed away from land, the full force of nature came to bear on the boat. The boatman rose to his element on the water, while Colclough the learned barrister was most definitely out of his.

Colclough began to cry on the Lord for protection on the waters in this storm on this day. But, the boatman said, he should not be praying on that side if he pleased; it was the other lad he ought to be praying to, in this situation. An alarmed Colclough asked what lad the boatman meant. 'What lad?' shouted the boatman into the searing wind, 'Why, sir, the auld people always say the Devil takes care of his own, and if you don't vex him by praying the other way, I really think, sir, I have a pretty safe cargo aboard on this present passage.'

And so it proved, for the boatman landed his charge safely on the other side and Colclough went on, in 1805, to be appointed Chief Justice of Prince Edward Island, one of the Atlantic provinces of Canada. His salary was £500 per annum, a sum that would have provided more than a few coins to compensate any ferryman for crossing stormy waters.

Someone who did indeed prevent people from passing her position beside a Wexford stream was the ghost of Petticoat Loose, and her story was recalled in the 1950s by eighty-five-year-old farmer John O'Neill of Ballinglee, to folklorist Jim Delaney of the Irish Folklore Commission.

Some Irish roads cross over streams and sometimes streams cross over roads; it all depends on the terrain and whatever is most convenient. Most times, a bridge of sorts takes man and beast dryshod over the water. However, in this particular place where Petticoat Loose appeared, the stream crossed the road. That was enough in itself to cause a traveller to pause on his journey, for we will all seek a way around or over water rather than splashing straight through it.

The fearsome ghost challenged all men that approached and demanded they call out their name to her. Dire consequences followed if the wrong name was given. It was known locally that if a challenged man jumped across the stream safely, she had no powers over him and he was safe. But if he did not manage that feat and the name he gave was the name she sought, then his end had arrived.

She had killed no less than three men up to the day that the man in the story hove into view. As it happened, his name was John and she soon made it clear to him that she only killed men named John.

John used all his reasoning to persuade the mad woman not to take away his life: he told her of all the good deeds he had done, and all he would do in the future if she would allow him pass her by without harm. When that did not impress her, he told her he was the son of parents and the parent of sons himself, and that he was a brother and a cousin and an uncle and any other relation he could imagine might lead her to a change of heart.

It did not persuade her from her declared intention of killing him, however. He offered her riches he did not possess to change her mind; but earthly riches impressed her less than his family responsibilities or his good works.

In the end, he sank to his knees and began to cry with outstretched hands, begging her to let him go. If she did, he said, he would return to her on the following night. He wanted to make peace with his family, he claimed, and his neighbours, his debtors and his creditors before his life ran its course. He promised he would return on the morrow to continue their conversation. This stratagem is well-known to the folklore of many lands; when a condemned man agrees to return in a day, or a year and a day, or some other agreed time-span, to be murdered having dealt with his duties in the time allotted.

She agreed to allow him to go and return on his word on the next day, when she would take his life. A trembling John crossed the stream and hurried to find a holy man, a priest, to advise him on what to do. The priest listened and asked questions and listened again, and finally he advised John to return and to keep his word to Petticoat Loose, lest he lose his own immortal soul, with his integrity compromised, for not keeping his word.

John returned on the agreed day. But this time while he spoke to her he remained on the safe side of the stream and did not jump across. Petticoat Loose was mad at that and said he promised to return. John replied that he had returned; but he had not said on which side of the water he would stand. He said he had a question to ask her: why did she kill only men named John?

She said she had killed an unbaptized child and had sinned against St John. However, she did not say which St John or why she wished to take the life of any man called John who came to her spot by the water's edge as a consequence. Try as he might, John could get no more from her and so returned to the priest to tell him what had occurred, and what he had learnt from his encounter with the mad woman called Petticoat Loose on the road beside the stream.

The priest called a meeting of all the priests that he could find and they sat and sat and sat for three days and three nights, discussing what they should do about this woman who had sinned against St John.

They were of the opinion, finally, that the killing of the child had left her soul in limbo and brought her to the place on the road where it must have taken place, and where she waited to take away the life of yet another victim. They decided, eventually, that they would banish her to a small island in the bay of Youghal Harbour in the neighbouring county of Cork. But, when she heard this, Petticoat Loose said that if they banished her, by whatever prayers and incantations they used to do so, she would wreck every ship that passed by the island.

The priests met again and decided instead to send her to the Red Sea, for it was the mouth of Hell, they believed, and there was no coming out of there for Petticoat Loose or anyone else banished there. This they did and she was never heard of again, according to farmer John O'Neill of Ballinglee.

However, another version of the same story as related by Kathleen Ronan of New Ross, a pupil in the Mercy Convent, in 1938 to teacher Sister Ni Mhaoldomhnaigh, said the victims were the mother and father, and two children (one without baptism), of Petticoat Loose herself. She herself died soon afterwards and on a dark night, not long after her death, her ghost appeared to a man riding by who took her up on the horse, as was the custom of the day. As soon as she settled on its back, the horse staggered under the sudden weight. The man remarked that he had never noticed the horse stagger like that before. She replied that the horse never carried such a weight of sins on its back before.

The man made her dismount and he journeyed home. In the morning he found the horse was dead. He mentioned the matter to a priest, who later visited the spot on the road where she had been left down. Petticoat Loose appeared in front of him and said she was here to kill any man who passed by.

He asked who sent her and she replied the Devil had sent her from Hell. She told the priest she was there for killing her mother and her father. He replied she could be shriven for that. But when she said she had also killed an unbaptized child, the priest said it was the killing of the child that had cursed her and banished her for ever.

So there she stayed; she may be there yet, waiting beside the stream that crosses the road in County Wexford.

Twenty-six

FLYING INTO
A HEDGE

Just a few days after the *Titanic* sank in the Atlantic, a couple
of amateur pilots were preparing for a slightly different
maiden voyage across water. They were hoping to pilot their
Bleriot XI monoplanes across the Irish Sea from England
to Ireland for the first time. An earlier attempt had been
made, in 1910, by Robert Loraine, a successful London and
Broadway stage actor and aviator. Flying a Farman biplane,
he had failed to reach Ireland by some 300 yards. He ditched
into the sea and swam the last few yards of his journey, but
since he did not bring his plane with him, his crossing was
not recognised, leaving the way clear for the two men in this
story to attempt the record.

Thirty-year-old Denys Corbett Wilson was an Edwardian
playboy, son of 'Carlos' Wilson, who used his barrister father's
fortune to excel in his pursuits of horse-racing, motor-racing
and, tragically for him, aeroplane-flying. His friend and avia-

tion rival was Irish-born Damer Leslie Allen. Wilson also had Irish connections; although born in Surrey on 24 September 1822, his mother was from County Kilkenny and the family returned there, to Darver House, Jenkinstown, when Wilson was seventeen.

Both men wanted to be the first reach their native land via the new mode of transport and there was a friendly rivalry between them – although there was no wager, as was generally believed at the time. The flight would be a tricky one, particularly for two such comparatively inexperienced pilots.

Both pilots set off from Hendon Aerodrome on Wednesday 16 April 1912. This was the same day the American aviator Harriet Quimbly became the first woman to fly the English Channel, making the crossing from Dover in England, to France in fifty-nine minutes.

Allen planned to fly to Ireland via Chester and Holyhead and so followed the track of the London and Northwestern Railway by way of direction and arrived at Chester about half-past six in the evening, said local reports.

Wilson, following a different route, landed the same evening at Almeley, some 15 miles north of Hereford, after mechanical failures caused him to crash-land in the meadow of Pentwyn Farm, Colva. Tradition has it that he had lost his compass and when he asked the first person he saw where he was, he was told, accurately enough, that he was in the top field.

On recovery of his breath and equilibrium, the moustachioed pilot saw that he had come down on the only piece of flat open ground available at Pentwyn Meadow. But if he thought he would be treated like a hero from the sky he was mistaken, for the plane had gouged lumps out of the meadow on its emergency landing. According to local folklore the irate farmer, unimpressed with such progress, told him to take his contraption away and to get out of his field.

Wilson was quite willing to oblige but could not do so with any alacrity. His aero mechanic had no other way to follow him but by steam train and he was somewhat behind the flying aeroplane by this time. Knowing that any delay would give Allen an advantage, Wilson decided not to wait for his mechanic to arrive and so bought oil locally for his engine the 80hp, seven-cylinder Gnome. This was his undoing, for Wilson, not knowing any better, lubricated his plane with castor oil and refuelled it with petrol siphoned from local agricultural machinery.

Once oiled and fuelled he set off again as soon as he could, wearing his woollen flying cap, goggles and fur-lined gloves to protect against the April elements in the open cockpit of his two-seater plane, which looked for all the world as if it had been made from spare bicycle parts and a balsa-wood frame.

Unsurprisingly, his engine did not recognise the concoction it was fed and, having taken off from the ground with great resolve, Wilson was forced to come down to land yet again, this time at Colva in Radnorshire.

Allen was by this stage well ahead. After an overnight stop at Chester, he set off at 6 o'clock the following morning and was observed passing 2 miles off Holyhead two hours later and heading out across the Irish Sea. Tragically, however, he was never to be seen again. He crashed into the sea and neither his body nor his plane was ever recovered. Sadly, the trip had been so hastily arranged that no precautions were made against the possibility of having to descend into the cold sea, and so no boats were on hand in case of an emergency landing. Allen was doomed when his plane went down.

Back in Radnorshire, Wilson's French mechanic, nineteen-year-old Gaston Vial, had finally caught up with him but it took Vial three days to clean the wrong fuel out of the engine and set it to rights once more.

Maddened farmers apart, Wilson was greeted with warmth by the people of Colva during his stay. A photograph of members of the local community with the aeroplane is preserved in some homes today, a unique memento of a moment in time that has passed into folklore. Naturally enough, the village children had the day off school to see the wonderful aeroplane that had come among them, and people walked for miles to witness the event – after all, it is not every day that a mechanical bird falls from the sky. On 22 April the plane was finally ready and the locals held it steady while Wilson revved the engine in preparation for his departure. More than a few were sorry to see him go and take his great adventure with him.

Airborne for the final time, Wilson headed for St George's Channel, Ireland, and Wexford once more. Conditions were reported to have been good until he was some 15 miles from the Wexford coast, when he ran into severe wind and rain. The rain and clouds made for poor visibility, nonetheless he finally spotted a field he thought suitable for landing a flying machine upon.

Wilson was flying over Crane, near Monageer, 2 miles from Enniscorthy when he spotted the field. Hoping there would be no complaining farmer to meet him this time, he made to land in the field. However, he soon ran out of grass and realised the landing strip was too short for his aircraft to come to a halt on; but by then he could do nothing about it. The bordering hedge approached at speed and the slim-bodied Bleriot XI monoplane ended up atop the hedge with a broken propeller. It could go no further, nor did it need to do any more, Ireland had been reached after just 100 minutes in the air.

Locals soon gathered around and asked him what he was doing, where he came from, and where did he think he was going, for the Wexford man and woman ever love a traveller with a story, especially one who has fallen from the sky with wings around him. Denys Corbett Wilson was delighted with the company and the reception, and once he found himself to be unhurt, he declared he was none the worse for his voyage.

He made arrangements for his aircraft to be repaired, took lodgings and, while waiting to be off, again became a celebrity in the district. He was brought in triumph to Enniscorthy and later reportedly flew a number of exhibition flights at the showgrounds. He made many friends locally before returning to his family home at Darver House in Jenkinstown, Kilkenny.

But dark clouds were gathering. On 13 May of the same year, King George V approved the formation of the Royal

Flying Corps as part of the British Army. The adventurous record-breaking Wilson signed up straightaway, even though he was of an age where he could have avoided serving in the armed forces.

Tragically, having survived the life-threatening inaugural flight over the Irish Sea, the fearless Denys Corbett Wilson was killed in the First World War. He died on 10 May 1915. By then a lieutenant serving in the Third Squadron, Royal Flying Corps, he and his observer were killed in action when their Morane Parasol aircraft was struck by German artillery while flying over their lines in France. His body is buried in the British war cemetery at Pas-de-Calais in France.

One week after Wilson's first crossing to Ireland, on 26 April, Vivian Hewitt successfully completed a flight between Holyhead and Dublin, landing on the 300 acres meadow at the heart of Phoenix Park, in the west of the city. The Welsh aviator had planned to fly to Ireland the day before Wilson's crossing, but was grounded by thick fog. When he managed to complete the crossing Hewitt took ten minutes off the days-old record, arriving in Dublin ninety minutes after take-off.

Twenty-seven

TOMFARNEY
LAND ATTACK

Land ownership and agrarian agitation run deep in the Irish psyche, no less so in County Wexford than in any other county. Passions often overflowed in the past with serious injury or death a consequence. In the 1830s, two men were hanged by the Crown for one such incident that typified the times. What was different about these hangings, however, was that one man said he was innocent and the other agreed with him, claiming all responsibility for himself.

A tithe was a tax levied on land that went to the support of the Church of Ireland clergy of the country. It was collected by proctors who were paid a percentage of what they collected. It was a particular cause of discontent to believers of other persuasions who had to hand over a tenth of their income to a minister of a religion they did not follow, while managing somehow to find the wherewithal to contribute to their own religion's upkeep.

Discontent simmered and church gates on Sundays were a natural meeting place for the high and low of society to exchange views. At one point, in 1796, a large multitude gathered at church gates and proceeded to Wexford to liberate two prisoners held there. They were members of one of the secret societies then agitating against the system. The people resolved to burn the town if their demand was not met. Tragically, a strong company of soldiers met them as they entered Wexford town. A desperate engagement ensued, according to contemporary reports, and many of the people in the crowd were killed or severely wounded. No military lives were lost, save for the officer in command who fell at the very beginning of the action. The untrained crowd was completely routed and failed to release their two companions. But discontent at the tithe and acts of disobedience were to continue throughout the county. The military was often called out to support the proctors in seizing goods or animals when the tithe was not paid. Loss of life sometimes followed.

In 1830, Catholic parishioners of Graiguenamanagh in County Kilkenny withheld their tithes and the inhabitants of Wexford and other counties quickly followed suit. At Bunclody, fourteen people were shot dead and many more injured by the yeomanry at one incident in June 1831. By 1832, the Tithe War had begun.

A public meeting held at Rathangan in 1832 petitioned against the payment of tithes. Others held at Blackwater and Olyegate demanded the same thing. Within a few years, stock seized for non-payment was put up for sale by auction at Brownswood, and at Ballyfad. Though thousands attended the sales, there were no bidders. And still the meetings continued with a large anti-tithe meeting being held in New Ross in 1836. By the following year, 1837, the amounts owing were large. Clement Rice, of Churchtown, Tagoat, was summoned to attend the assizes at the Court House, Wexford, as a juror. However, once there he was arrested for non-payment of tithes and costs amounting to some £100, and lodged in gaol for his sins.

Tragically, the war was to become more violent and on Saturday 2 March 1833 two Wexford men, John Redmond and Nicholas Jackman, went on trial before Baron Foster for the murder, on 22 November 1832, of policeman Joseph Wright, a married man from Glynn, and Mary Madock and her daughter at Tomfarney, in the barony of Bantry and county of Wexford.

John Redmond's father had occupied a farm at Tomfarney but he was dispossessed for non-payment of rent and it was taken by the Edmund Madock family. However, shortly after Madock took possession he received threatening notices. Two policemen were stationed at his house for protection by the authorities, who were determined the law should stand. But the house was attacked by an armed party of up to fifty men. They surrounded the house and set fire to it. Eight people were in the house at the time, most of whom had gone to bed, when smoke began to spread through the living quarters.

The choking policemen opened the door to relieve the situation. They were met by a volley of shots from outside. Constable Joseph Wright fell to the ground, mortally wounded. A second volley was fired at the house, which caused the death of Mrs Mary Madock and her daughter Margaret. Edmund Madock was severely wounded and his son received two musket balls to the chest, but both survived.

Other members of the household escaped, including another of Madock's sons who was to become the principal witness. He concealed himself under some bushes until all was quiet again. Later discovered by the police, he was held in protective custody until the trial began. Damage done, the attackers dispersed but they were followed by the military and police, and it was not long until they were arrested.

John Redmond and Nicholas Jackman were accused of the murder and lodged in the county gaol to await their trial. They were tried at the following March Assizes and found guilty. On being asked if they had anything to say as to why sentence of death by execution should not be passed on them, Nicholas Jackman caused a sensation when he responded with deathly passion.

He said that whatever time he might part this life, the Kingdom of Heaven or the sight of God might he never see if he was out of his house for half an hour on the night of the attack on the house of the Madocks. He said that if the jury, or any lord on this earth, found him guilty, he would leave his innocent blood on them.

While the stunned court was contemplating such a promised and terrible curse, his co-accused stepped forward. John Redmond, in a firm and audible voice, said he was the killer, not only of the Madocks, but of John Roche of Old Court, who had been killed in a separate attack. Redmond said Nicholas Jackman who stood by his side, as well as James Jackman, who was found guilty the day before of the murder of Roche, were innocent. Nonetheless, Redmond and Jackman were sentenced to be executed on the following Monday 4 March. The prisoners were removed, under a large armed escort, to the county gaol, and a strong military guard was kept there until after the execution.

(James Jackman had been found guilty of aiding and assisting at the murder of John Roche of Old Court and was sentenced, at a separate hearing, to hang on 4 March, but was granted respite until the 25th. His sentence was then commuted to transportation for life, and he was removed from Wexford gaol on 28 March.)

The owner of the *Wexford Independent* newspaper, a Mr Greene, was allowed to interview the condemned men. Still protesting his innocence, Jackman fell on his knees before Greene and in the most solemn manner, called on Him who knows the secrets of all hearts, to witness the truth of what he said.

Redmond, on the other hand, told Greene that he was not sorry for what he did, and if he had the power he would commit the same deeds over again; that he would as soon die then as a month hence, as life had no charms for him. He declared he had got the retribution he desired for the wrongs inflicted on his father.

Nonetheless, innocent or guilty, both men were hanged until they expired, according to their sentence.

For agrarian agitators they received quite a comprehensive religious send-off. They were attended by the Revd Aidan Devereux, who afterwards became first Bishop of the Cape of Good Hope; the Revd Dr Sinnott, President of St Peter's College, Wexford; the Revd John Barry, afterwards parish priest of Crossabeg; and the Revd Laurence Kirwan, the Dean of Ferns.

Refusing to be hanged as a guilty man, Jackman, when he came to the gallows, declared his innocence. He knelt down and prayed fervently. He became so weak in the effort that he had to be carried up to the scaffold, a wooden structure erected on the gaol green, some few yards from the entrance gate, to be executed by the hangman.

Again, Redmond acknowledged his guilt and declared Jackman to be innocent, but to no avail. John Redmond was the youngest of seven brothers, and was aged less than twenty years when he died at Wexford gaol.

The Tithe Commutation Act of 1838, which came too late for Redmond and Jackman, reduced tithes and converted them to a fixed rent charge. This placed responsibility on the landlord who, where possible, added the charge to the rent a tenant had to pay.

Shortly after this, the Great Famine of the 1840s hurled more depredations on the people. It forced millions from the land when the potato crop failed and income fell so low as to make payment of rents impossible. Starvation followed and a mass migration of people ensued, creating folklore and stories of tragedy and resistance throughout the county and country. For where land lies in Ireland, passion and story abide.

Twenty-eight

TRAGEDY AT SEA ON ST MARTIN'S EVE

Wherever people live by the sea, stories of tragedies will come ashore to haunt the living. In Wexford a fishing tragedy of some 300 years ago is still remembered today, and is likely to be passed from one generation to the next for some time to come.

As many as seventy families lost relatives in the month of November in the early 1700s, in what could best be described as extraordinary circumstances including forewarnings, pleas to fishermen not to put to sea, apparitions, ghostly warnings and mass drownings.

To this day, St Martin's feast day on 11 November each year is a day on which no Wexford fishing boat will put to sea.

The tragedy began on the evening before, when fishermen saw that a shoal of herring had come to Wexford Bay and they put out to reap the harvest – despite strident warnings not to.

The herring fishery had been so great about the year 1654, a mere few generations earlier, that more than 80,000 barrels of herring were entered in the custom house records for the year. It was said that over 40,000 barrels more were filled that were not entered in the official records at Wexford, at all. However, the trade was in decay, so much so that by 1678, two decades later, a mere 200 barrels were entered in the records and by 1682, not even 200 barrels were made in the whole year.

However, the Irish fishing industry was still strong enough in 1698 for two petitions to be presented to the House of Commons from the fishermen of Folkstone and other English ports, stating their livelihood was injured by the Irish fishermen catching herring at Waterford and Wexford, and sending them to markets, thereby forestalling and ruining the petitioners' markets. They said that there was sometimes to be seen at Wexford some 200 sail of vessels – English, French and Dutch – taking in fish cargoes from the Irish waters. Laws were issued, as a consequence, forbidding any Irish to appear out of harbour or fish while English fishermen were so engaged.

Some of which might explain why Wexford fishermen were anxious to put to sea when opportunity arose on St Martin's Eve in the early 1700s. In earlier times, much of Western Europe, including Ireland, engaged in fasting beginning on St Martin's Day, 11 November. This fast period lasted forty days. (This period of fasting was later shortened and called Advent.) St Martin's Eve was, therefore, the last opportunity for people to eat and drink fully before they started to fast. A ritual was observed in many parts of the country of having a feast. Those who could afford it would kill a sheep; those of lesser means would kill a fowl. The sacrifice was segregated a week before the night of its departure from this world. The head of the house did the killing and the blood was then sprinkled in all four corners of the house, and on the door posts on the threshold, to observe the niceties of the night and to pay respect to the saint.

It was also the tradition in Ireland for no wheel to be turned on St Martin's Day because the saint had been killed by being thrown into a mill stream and killed by the wheel. This meant that no milling or sewing of any kind could be done. Nor could any sailing boats put to sea.

Poet John Boyle O'Reilly wrote about the night in his 1878 poem 'The Fishermen of Wexford'. He relates how, on that particular day, the wondrous shoal of herring arrived in the waters of the bay. Fishermen and their families stood on the beach and all day watched with wistful eyes the wealth they might not reach because of custom and practice. Such a shoal had never before been seen, they said, as they regretted their constrictions of custom.

When they could stay away no longer, some fishermen headed for their boat and soon the strand was filled with the grating sound of boats' keels on shingle as, one by one, the fishing boats entered the water to begin taking in the herring.

Fear ran through the women who were present when they realised the fishermen of Wexford meant to sail on St Martin's Eve. Wives, daughters, nieces, cousins and sweethearts cried out for the men to stay away from the water as they would not be back before midnight. White-haired men joined in the chorus, saying to their sons, grandsons and nephews that this thing had never been done and no good would come of it. They said the fishermen were tempting the Lord. But the seamen said the Lord never sent a shoal of fish except as a reward to a fisherman. They said that night that their nets would catch all that was in the bay, and threatened that they would even take the saint who guarded it, should they come across him.

The moon shone brightly on the sea and the faces of those assembled on the shore, as seaward went the fishing boats and heavenward went the cries of keening wives and mothers. The wailing women cried to the Holy Virgin to be their guard. The old men, now sad and silent, watched the boats pass the farthest headland, beyond the lighthouse as, in a line, they went to meet the fish.

The briny was lit by phosphorous, said John Boyle O'Reilly in his poem, as the fishing-fleet went seaward. All the while, prayers were offered from the shore to save the wilful men from the wrath they had surely roused by their avaricious greed.

The boats reached a good location and nets were thrown out. But hearts ashore were chilled to hear the wind begin to moan. The nets had scarcely sunk an inch below the surface when the boatmen on the water were astonished at what they saw rising from the sea before them. It was a human shape arising from the sea, warning them with upraised hand to go back to land.

It fell away below them into the fathoms of water. As they watched, it gleamed whitely through the water, and frowned up at them, its white hand clenched, before vanishing beneath the waves. But fear was soon forgotten at the sensation of rushing herring beneath the boats and, defying the dreadful warning, they steered their boats after the fish and wildly hauled on the nets.

But before they could bring the fish into their boats, a huge storm arose behind and before them. The wind roared and waves washed over their boats, swamping them and throwing the fishermen into the sea. No one was saved. That was the version of the story put forward by John Boyle O'Reilly.

Another was recorded by schoolteacher Brigid Ní Eadhra of Fethard while she was working in Loftus Hall school in Templeton. On the night in question, one boat was a man short. The rest of the crew waited an hour for him to turn up but he did not show. A stranger came down the quay and agreed to join them in their quest for herring. Once out, they had good catch hauled in when the stranger said they should turn for home for a storm was coming, and they best be safe ashore when it arrived. He also told his surprised companions that a man would be standing on the quay with a white horse near the ring bolt they needed to tie their boat to. He said the man would offer to help them moor and ask them to throw him their rope; the stranger warned that if they agreed to the request they would be lost.

When they reached the harbour the fisherman did indeed see the man and his white horse. However, instead of throwing the rope to him, their new fishing companion jumped ashore himself and securely made the rope fast. The fishermen were busy with their catch, readying it to be unloaded, and when they looked up they were astonished to find that their new companion and the stranger with the white horse had vanished, never to be seen again.

The storm, when it came ashore, lasted all night. Afterwards, people said the stranger was St Martin and the horseman the Devil.

In the days that followed that terrifying night, the sea gave up its dead one at a time until, when the counting was done, there were lifeless corpses of seventy fishermen strewn along the shores of Wexford, while the wives and mothers, sweethearts, and white-haired men who had cried, stop mourned for the loss of so many fine fishermen of Wexford.

The story of their foolishness has been told by one generation to the next as a warning not to disregard the wisdom and weight of custom passed through the times, one to the other. Seventy souls were lost that night and not one fish was brought ashore by any of them.

Twenty-nine

SEA
STORIES

Wexford is bounded by the sea on two sides: on the south by the Atlantic Ocean and on the east by St George's Channel and the Irish Sea. It is not then surprising that Wexford folklore has brought us many stories of the sea and the people that went down to the sea: some to return, some never to leave it, except in their spectral forms.

Along the east coast at Arklow, Courtown and other seaside villages the seas are not ordinarily as rough as the Atlantic to the south, but sand banks off the coast were often the death trap of sailing ships before the coming of sonar soundings recorded warnings.

The tapering headland of Hook Head in the south-western corner of County Wexford has featured in sea stories for hundreds of years. One such tale dates from at time when no town had the right to call itself the capital of the island, for all towns were growing, or declining, in their own way.

A powerful woman wanted to make Ross the capital of Ireland. She had three sons and, like every Irish mother that ever was, she had high hopes for them becoming men of influence. For this to happen and to achieve her ambition of forming a new capital, she sent her three lads out on three ships. They were to sail all over the world and collect enough wealth to bring home three ships full of gold to pay for building the capital city.

Seasons came and went, and they travelled all the known seas trading, buying and selling, and when all was done to their satisfaction, they turned to sail safely home with the treasure they had accumulated.

There was no lighthouse on Hook Head at that time, so their mother went there and put up a storm light, up high, so they could see where they were and to prevent them crashing into the rock and losing all. But the returning sons had been away for such a long time that, by the time they reached the Wexford coast, on a dark moonless night, the light had gone out. Unable to see any landmarks, they came in at Hook Head – thinking they were at Ross harbour – and tried to come ashore. The first brother's ship struck the point and foundered, losing all. This was followed, one at a time, by his brothers' ships, the crews and cargoe.

On hearing the news, the now-childless mother abandoned the idea of making Ross the capital of Ireland and set herself to grieve for her three fine sons now lying at the bottom of the sea.

They were not the only ones to perish on that part of the coast. According to a later tradition, the monks of St Dubhan kept alight a beacon to warn sailors of the dangers of shipwreck on the rocky headland. Nonetheless, ships and lives continued to be lost up and down the Wexford coast.

Apart from legitimate traders mistaking one place for another and running aground, there was also a deal of smuggling going on along the Wexford coast. A story is recorded in

the Irish Folklore Commission Collection of an occurrence at Barrow Bay some time in the 1830s. It was a time when a lot of smuggling was going on in Bannow and Blackhall. One evening, a vessel came into Barrow Bay and anchored. The captain came ashore from his ship in a small boat and said he was looking for a cargo of potatoes to buy. He made no attempt to bring in the vessel to land but came in himself every day. He mingled with the people he met, making much of himself and of them. One day, he invited many of the locals to come to a big supper in the vessel at anchor that evening. He had become friendly with the Coastguard for the area and he invited that worthy to the supper too. The Coastguard could not go but he sent his son and daughter in his stead. All in all, the whole party that went out amounted to thirty souls. All were happy enough going and those that remained behind wished them well as they left.

However, when morning came there was no sign of the ship or the local people who had rowed out to her the evening before with such conviviality.

A few days afterwards, the bodies of all thirty were washed up on the strand between Bannow Church and Bannow Island. Of the ship or its captain there was no sign, then or ever since.

William Cox from Duncormick reported another incident. He was going down to the water on a night when there was a strong gale blowing in from the sea. He thought no boat could travel at all in such a sea, but a ship passed by going like a steamer, as if the Devil was in her that night. Later on, he found the headless body of a man washed up on the shore. William thought he might from the *Brother Jonathan* or the *Kate Kearney* which had both foundered recently with the loss of all aboard. The body was buried at Cullenstown graveyard and the next night a light was seen to appear at the place the body came ashore, and travel across to the graveyard; William supposed it meant the poor sailor was at rest.

Tales abound of strange occurrences witnessed by people in extremis on the sea. In 1915, during the First World War, a ship was seen off Greenore Point steaming towards land at speed. Observers recognised it as a warship, and the crew of a tugboat that was in the area at the time hoisted colours for identification purposes. The oncoming vessel did not respond to her signal, which was the first sign that there was something strange about her. The crew of the tug boat passed near enough to see there were figures on her deck, but they did not respond to signals. The warship remained steady on her course and the tug boat headed to Tuskar lighthouse to discuss the strange behaviour of the ship with the lighthouse keepers. But the lighthouse keepers said no warship had passed the Tuskar that morning. Still, the full crew of the tugboat had seen her with their own eyes and had stood on deck as she passed them by on the sea.

The sighting became another mystery of the sea around the coast of Wexford. It compares to the stories of a boat being seen from time to time heading into the Skellig Islands. The boat is seen leaving the mainland with people on it but it never reaches the island, nor passes the island on the way out to sea. Local boatmen seem unconcerned about the sightings for they say the boat will harm nobody as it sails about its business.

Captain Curran of Irishtown, New Ross, reported an adventure of his own on a voyage in the 1880s, which he told to James Power of the Madlins. The story was, in turn. collected by Mary B. Dunphy, a teacher in a school in Irishtown in 1938. The story now forms part of the Irish Folklore Commission Collection. In mid-ocean Captain Curran reported that he came on a vessel that did not return the usual marine salutation. Curran steered closer still, flying his signal. Receiving no answer, he came to the belief that her crew was taken ill and needed help. He let down his lifeboat and he and a member of his own crew rowed to the silent ship and went aboard.

Everything was in perfect order as they moved through the ship, but of the crew there was no trace. They searched for clues as to what had happened to remove all sight of a human form from the ship, but none were found.

Captain Curran returned to his own vessel and appointed the mate of his own ship as captain of the mystery vessel. Both vessels arrived in port safe and sound and Captain Curran and all connected to the retrieval of the ship were paid salvage by the Board of Trade for their work.

A few years before Curran's discovery, Richard Griffith Noble Heard, Chief Inspector of the Coastguards, survived the wreck of the *Ceres*. The *Ceres*, a steamer with sails, was sailing from Plymouth to Dublin with twenty-nine passengers and nine crew when it struck the shore near Carnsore Point on the evening of 10 November 1866. The vessel was about 20 miles off course at the time.

As the ship found itself in among the breakers in the winter darkness, the passengers assembled in the saloon and on their knees commended their souls to God's care, for they believed their end was come. The waves struck the vessel, smashing the woodwork, and water flooded into the saloon. The ship was not far off the coast of Wexford and so they fired blue emergency flares. The flares were seen and rescue was attempted from the land. Some of those aboard made it to the beach from the wrecked ship by scaling down a rope thrown down for the purpose; others were carried off by the waves.

A number of men survived, including Mr Heard the Chief Inspector of the Coastguards, but only one woman and one child made it off the ship alive.

In a subsequent enquiry the captain, who also survived, said the wreck was caused by the on-board compasses going astray.

In another famous incident off the coast of Wexford, the *John A. Harvey*, a new three-masted barquentine carrying a cargo of yellow corn, was caught off Kilmore on a lee shore and could not free itself. The crew cut the masts down and they fell overboard on the leeside, according to a man by the name of J. Devereux who heard the account of what happened from his mother, who was a native of Kilmore. However, the crew did not cut the masts clean away so the masts and rigging hung over the lee rail; the lifeboat, in consequence, could not get near the ship and the crew could not come off.

There they stayed until the following day, when the storm eased a deal. A lifeboat went out again and this time managed to get the crew off and took them safely ashore. Amazingly, no lives were lost. They were the lucky ones, for although the sea off Wexford can be calm and restful, it can also be angry and dangerous. It behoves man to pay it due respect.

Thirty

SEA
PEOPLE

The story of the seal woman who comes ashore to marry a human and who for ever afterwards pines for the sea is common among most nations with a shoreline. Wexford has its own version of the story of a Moruach, the name given to the sea-maidens that swim in the shallow waters near our coasts.

While seamaidens are said to be breathtakingly beautiful and instantly capable of stealing away the heart of any man who chances upon them, seamen, or mermen as they are called in some places, do not seem to be an attractive or interesting class of being. Their hair and teeth are green, their noses are red, and their eyes resemble those of a pig: not attributes designed to attract most people. Moreover, they have a liking for brandy and keep a look-out for cases of that drink that have gone astray, from time to time, in shipwrecks off the Wexford coast. It is no wonder then, that their females occasionally look to the land for some male company, for beauty is in the eye of the beholder and faraway men are handsome.

In the folklore of many cultures, the female wears a light skin that she can remove to move about the land in human form when she comes ashore. It is this skin that the infatuated mortal manages to take possession of and hide, with the consequence that the seamaiden must stay with him until, if ever, he returns the skin to her so that she can swim away once more, to join her own people in their natural environment. In most stories she recovers the skin – even if it is years later and children have been born to the union. She leaves the mortal world to the distress of the human husband who thought she was with him for the rest of their lives. Unusually for a mother-and-child story, she also leaves behind their offspring to fend for themselves as best they can.

The Wexford version of the story says that the wearing of a magic cap rather than a light outer skin is essential to a sea-maiden's well-being in her world below the waves. Once the cap is removed ashore, the sea maiden appears to be entirely human. Nonetheless, a mortal husband must keep this cap well concealed from his sea-wife, lest her desire to swim to sea become unbearable and she be away to swim with the fishes.

Instances are rife of desolation wrought in families by the unintentional finding of the magic cap by one of the children, who shows it to her mother and asks her what it is. However strong her affection for husband and children, she is instinctively obliged to seize on it and clap it on her head, according to Kilmyshall-born story collector Patrick Kennedy who gathered the Wexford version of the story in the 1800s. The departing mother tenderly embraces her children, but flies to the sea shore nonetheless, then plunges in and is seen no more. The distracted husband, when he hears the news from the forsaken children, calls for aid to the powers of sea and land, but in vain. Why did he perpetrate an unsuitable marriage he asks, to no response? He spends his time ever after in mourning for his loss.

It happened that one man, who lived near Bantry in County Wexford, was blessed with an excellent wife from among the Moruach, though how she came ashore or where they first met, or how he managed to remove her cap from her head to render her landbound, is not told. He was a snug farmer and his home was built into a slope of a hill for protection from the elements. A small orchard of a few trees and a cabbage-garden and a haggard lay at the back of the dwelling. The barn, a cow-house and a stable enclosed three sides of the place. The fourth was bounded by a low white wall, with a black iron gate to come and go by in its centre.

It happened that the mornings at this time of the year were beginning to have a damp feel about them; the leaves on trees in the county had turned yellow and brown, and fell and lay strewn along the roads in and about the place. The winds coming in off the sea had a mournful sound as they whistled through the thinly covered branches of large trees. They carried the tang of salt water with them, a powerful aphrodisiac and calling for any sea creature. The Moruach grew restless as she always did at this time of the year when the sea called her home.

Otherwise, the pair lived comfortably and were content, and if the seamaiden pined for her marine cap the farmer was wise enough to keep it well hidden from her, for he had no wish to lose his wife to the sea. For once a Moruach swam away she would not return to earthly form of her own free will; once fooled into a life on the land she knew the danger of conversing with a mortal.

In this case, however, a number of sea-cows that were aware of his wife's original incarnation as a seamaiden persisted in coming up to graze on her husband's meadows that were close to the shoreline, so as to be near their own. She understood what was happening and what they were saying to her, but turned away.

Sadly, while the husband was a loving partner well pleased with his sea-wife and the delights she brought him, he was otherwise an unsentimental man, not given to indulging anything that would intrude on his life or the life of his family. When he saw the sea-cows beached on their bellies on his land, he chased and worried the animals back into the sea once more, hitting them and inflicting bruises when they did not move fast enough for his liking.

His sea-wife, seeing this with her own eyes and hearing stories while he was not there from her friends among the sea people, asked him to stop hurting the sea animals. But he continued to drive them off, in spite of her entreaties. Why he did so, or whether it was from territoriality or fear of what might happen to his family if they swayed his wife's feelings, is impossible to tell at this remove.

What is certain is that the seamaiden could take it no longer and one day, while he was away at market, she searched the house, high and low, until she found what she was seeking – everything comes to those that look long enough for what they want. She found the small cap that had been hidden from her for so long. It fitted her head snugly, even still. So, she slipped away while her children were otherwise engaged and went to the water's edge. She paused for a moment between the mortal world and the world of the sea people, before sinking slowly into the water and beneath the waves. She was home.

The farmer was distraught and regretted his actions when he found she was no longer with him. If he could have swapped his abuse of the sea-cows for his wife's company he would gladly have done so. But, like many a mortal, he was sorry when it was too late. He stood on the shore every evening and studied the water to see if she would re-appear, but he never saw again.

The only memento he had of her was that their children, and theirs again, and probably theirs again unto the present day, were distinguished by a rough scaly skin and a delicate membrane between fingers and toes that few earthbound mortals shared. It was the only memory they had that their mother had been a Moruach from the sea. It was piece of family history they shared with few people.

Curiously enough, there is another story, from the southern end of the country, of someone driving a family of cattle into the sea through violence and abuse. Several centuries earlier than this Moruach story, a family that lived on Durzy Island found a beautiful coal-black bull and a cow on a green spot near the beach, and brought them home to await their owner's call for them to be restored to him. Time passed and since nobody called for them nor sought them, they became that family's property. The cow furnished sufficient butter and milk for all domestic desires, and when the bull fulfilled his part of the bargain a calf was in due course added to their number, the following year. In turn, this youngster came to the age of affording additional support to the family.

All went well until the day a wicked servant girl beat the mother cow in a fit of temper. On that day, while milking the cow, she so far forgot herself as to strike the uncomplaining beast with the spancel she had used to hobble the cow with while she milked her. Not content with striking the poor cow, the servant girl also cursed her bitterly for needing to be milked when she would rather have been doing anything else. The outraged animal turned around to the other two, the bull and the calf, who were grazing at some distance away, and lowed to them in a sorrowful tone. While the astonished maidservant watched helplessly, all three moved away at a trot and travelled rapidly to the sea. They plunged into the water, and, according to the folklore of the area, three rocks, known afterwards as the Bull, Cow, and Calf, arose from the sea.

Where the bull and the cow came from in the first place is not known, nor even if they were in some way attached to the sea at all, but it is curious to reflect on the fact that both stories have their catalyst in the mistreatment of cattle beside the sea and, in both cases, the sea became their refuge from the hand of man.

Thirty-one

GOING
AWAY

If you live in a sea-bordering county, it is not surprising that you might take to the sea and emigrate for a better life when all other options are denied to you. Many Wexford people have prospered in their new country; though some did not do so well and might have been better off saving the price of the ticket.

Some went on to dominate the sea they sailed upon. John Barry, father of the American Navy, was born the son of a poor tenant farmer who was evicted from a cottage in 1745 at Our Lady's Island, County Wexford. He started his own working life as a ship's cabin boy, and graduated through the ranks to head the new navy of the United States of America.

In the following century an old woman, Catherine Somers, had three sons out in America. They had gone out around the 1880s, according to Matthew Rowe, a retired farmer of Wexford who was himself eighty-seven years of age when he passed the story on to folklorist James Delaney, in 1955. The story is to be found in the Irish Folklore Collection.

Before heading off on their great adventure, the Somers boys held a hooley as most Irish people did before they emigrated. Parting Sprees, as they were called in parts of Wexford, were usually held on the Sunday night before the emigrants left Ireland. There was dancing, music and singing, storytelling and trick acting at these sprees where there was also plenty of drink to be had to wet the emigrant's head for the journey. Such a party would start at about seven in the evening in winter time, but later in the summer. It was held in the house of the emigrant and he and his family supplied the provisions for the party. There was a formal supper, consisting of tea, bread and butter and strong drink was given out to all and sundry. Any friends or neighbours who wanted to attend were welcome to do so, as were any workers there might be on the farm. The party went on till about two o'clock in the morning, most times, but ended then, for Monday was a day of work for those not going to America.

After a brief sleep, the boys climbed aboard their pony and trap and set off on their long journey to a distant shore. They dressed in simple second-hand clothes, so as to save money for when they got to America (corduroy breeches, a white shirt with a high collar, clean stockings, an old hat and a long-swallow-tailed coat over all). They each also carried a small pinch of salt, tied in a paper, for it was well known that any person carrying salt would not be touched by evil on his journey.

Once settled in America, the boys were keen to send word to their mother to keep her and their friends back home up to date with their news, and also to send her any money they could spare. However, here they hit upon a snag, for, although they had each attended school and learned the rudiments of reading and writing, none of them were able to write an entire letter. This was a problem faced by many Irish emigrants and, luckily, the problem had already been solved by professional writers who set themselves up in business and who, for a small fee or other appropriate payment, would write the dictated letter out, ready to be sent.

A similar system had to be set up in Ireland for those who received the letters, for few of the emigrants' kin could read. Those of the professional classes – doctors, teachers, solicitors, priests – were called upon to read the letters for the recipients. Some liked their letters read to them privately, but many organised public recitations. After all, it saved them having to endlessly repeat their news to the many curious neighbours who would want to know the latest once word had gone round the village that a letter from America had arrived.

Mrs Somers was one of those people who could not read or write, and so whenever she got a letter she would ask the local schoolteacher, John Doyle, to come and read it to her and her assembled neighbours. When Doyle saw the first letter sent by Mrs Somers' son, he commented on the fine penmanship, far different from the writing style the Somers boys had exhibited when they attended his school. Mrs Somers confidently explained this away by saying that they were writing in American now, and that was why it was different.

Jim Brien, a local man, always attended any letter-reading sessions in the village. He would sit as close as possible to Doyle and watch the words on the page that were being read out, as best he could. In this way, he formed a familiarity with the way letters were written to be read. He would nod knowledgeably as the teacher read and soon people began to believe that Jim Brien could also read.

Mrs Somers' boys, Sean, James and Terence, took it in turns to compose the letters they sent back to Ireland, for they all had their own stories to tell. Even though they were members of the same family and close siblings, they had different points of view on everything. One day, a letter arrived and Mr Doyle was not available to read it as he was away visiting his sister, so when Jim Brien stooped his head to come into the house he was told he was needed to read the letter.

Jim could see no way out but to pretend that he could read and to make the letter up as he went along. If any anomalies turned up afterwards he could always blame the light from the paraffin lamp, where the wick was in need of trimming. So he took the letter and began to 'read', telling his assembled audience of the weather and the conditions in America, which he knew of from other letters he had heard anyway. But Mrs Somers grew impatient at the son that had written home to say nothing at all so she asked Jim to state which of the boys it was from.

Jim, of course, did not know and he evaded the question by saying he had not reached the end of the letter yet. By the time he got to the foot of the page, with no news at all out of the Somers boy, his inspiration began to fail and Jim started to stammer as if the words were rolling around the page on their own. Far from being perturbed by this turn of events, the old woman smiled when she heard Jim stammering and said that she now knew who it was from. She said it was from her youngest son, Terry, the one that always had a stoppage in his speech. A relieved Jim said the impediment must have carried over into his writing since he went to America, so.

All marvelled at this phenomenon and wondered how it could come about. They marvelled anew at the skill of the reader who was so able to catch the voice of the tormented writer beyond in America. The schoolteacher, when next called to read a letter from Terry, was advised of the stammering writing of his former pupil and wondered, not for the first time, if everyone he had taught in that village school had cracked afterwards under the strain of living in this community, for it was deadly hard to find one sane person among them all.